**Rachel Dove** is a tutor and romance/romcom author from West Yorkshire in the UK. She lives with her husband and two sons, and dreams of a life where housework is done by fairies and she can have as many pets as she wants. When she's not writing or reading she can be found walking her American cocker spaniel, Oliver, in the great outdoors, or dreaming of her next research trip away with the family.

*Fighting for the Trauma Doc's Heart*

is **Rachel Dove**'s debut title

Look out for more books
from Rachel Dove
coming soon

Discover more at millsandboon.co.uk.

# FIGHTING FOR THE TRAUMA DOC'S HEART

RACHEL DOVE

MILLS & BOON

First published in Great Britain 2020
by Mills & Boon, an imprint of HarperCollins*Publishers*
1 London Bridge Street, London, SE1 9GF

Large Print edition 2021

© 2020 Rachel Dove

ISBN: 978-0-263-28756-1

MIX
Paper from
responsible sources
FSC
www.fsc.org
FSC™ C007454

This book is produced from independently certified FSC™ paper to ensure responsible forest management. For more information visit www.harpercollins.co.uk/green.

Printed and bound in Great Britain
by CPI Group (UK) Ltd, Croydon, CR0 4YY

This book is dedicated to all the parents and carers out there fighting for their child's place in the world, and to my sons. Thanks for sharing your neurodiverse world with me. *I love you to the moon and back, and all the stars in between.*

# CHAPTER ONE

MICHELLE FORBES WAS barely out of her car when she saw the ambulance pull into the bay at the front of the hospital's main doors. St Marshall's had another entrance for trauma, but that was around the other side. This couldn't be good.

Slamming her car door, she threw her backpack over her shoulders and thrust her keys into her coat pocket, pulling out a bottle of hand sanitiser and running straight to the ambulance. Dousing her hands in the alcohol solution, she shoved the bottle back into her pocket and greeted the two men pulling the gurney out of the back of the ambulance doors.

'What've we got?' she demanded, reaching for a pair of gloves from one of the rig's shelves before following them in.

'Welcome back. Female, twenty-seven, found unconscious at the scene of an RTA.'

They rushed through the main doors, shouting at people to get out of the way as they ran the gauntlet of the main reception area, heading right to the trauma wing. A medic she knew—Bradley—did a double-take when he saw her, but then it was straight back to business.

'We have two other ambulances incoming: an elderly couple, both awake and responsive at the scene, and one unconscious pregnant woman. Thirty-two weeks along. Her ETA is approximately ten minutes; they were cutting her out of the car when we left. This one—' the paramedic pointed at the unconscious woman as they ran hell for leather towards the nearest bay '—is a cyclist. Her helmet was on but not fastened. It came off in the collision. Her breathing is stable. Possible fractured pelvis, right broken forearm. She hit her head on the tarmac as she landed. No consciousness since, but pupils are equal and reactive.'

'Right.' Michelle nodded, jabbing at the door button as they hit the bay.

She noticed her hands were shaking slightly, but when she clenched her fists tight and then unfurled them it stopped. Heads turned as she barrelled through, barking orders as she went. Michelle commanded any room she walked into, and she had long since forgotten to be sorry about that, even now.

'Check for any other bleeding and call for a CT scan immediately. We need to check on that head. Get Ortho up here to assess these fractures, and I'll come back to reset them myself once we have the scans. Page OB and Ortho—tell them we have incoming traumas.'

Bradley gave her a curt nod and got to work.

The whole trauma centre came to life as she spoke to the room. If Dr Forbes spoke, you damn well listened. Out of respect, mostly. She didn't work on fear; she had seen its effects too many times to value it as any sort of teaching aid.

'Clear the beds, people! Three traumas incoming. One thirty-two weeks pregnant and unconscious. Two elderly people, awake and responsive. Bed Two is stable, unconscious, and has multiple fractures. Check them in, people, and check them out!'

She headed for the on-call room, grabbing a pair of fresh scrubs from the pile kept in there. Within seconds she was dressed and ready to go. Talk about a gentle easing back in to the day job. *Sheesh.*

She went to open the door, but froze when she heard her name being mentioned. She held her hands out in front of her, grateful to see that they were as steady as a rock now.

*It must have been the adrenaline*, she thought to herself. *I'm back. I can do this. I want to be here. Here grounds me. Normality. Work. Friends. Just got to keep it together. Fake it till you make it, Doctor.*

'Shh—not the time!'

One of the nurses was trying to silence a porter Michelle recognised—Alan. He'd worked in trauma for years and was one of her favourite colleagues. Fast, quick, and he got the job done. Just the kind of person every head of trauma wanted to have working for her.

'We have trauma incoming—just leave it!'

Michelle opened the door just a crack more, giving herself half a second to listen in. Alan seemed rattled, and that made her Spidey senses tingle. One thing she had learned from her tours as a medic: you listened to your gut. Helping charitable organisations overseas and working with the army had taught her that staying alive meant being true to your own instincts and having the courage to see your plan through.

'It's not fair, though,' Alan hissed into the nurse's ear. 'She went to help her fellow countrymen and this is what she gets? We don't need any more change around here; I don't like it. I really don't like lying to her, either.'

The nurse didn't get the chance to reply as Michelle swept out through the door, shutting it firmly behind her, having stashed her backpack under one of the beds.

'Michelle!' Alan said smoothly, and any reservation that might have shown on his face was shrouded carefully by his friendly open smile. 'Glad you're back.'

She smiled, tapping him on the shoulder. She could hear the incoming ambulances and was already back to thinking about work. Whatever that was all about, it would come out in the wash soon enough. Even in a large hospital like this gossip never stayed secret for long. No need for her to get involved.

'Glad to be back. I hope you haven't wrecked the place!' she called over her shoulder as she ran to the trauma centre doors.

Two ambulances came screeching to a halt, one after the other, and medics were already scrambling to help. Michelle burst through the doors and was at the door to the first ambulance when she was almost hit by one of the doors flying open, with a shouting man behind it.

'Trauma, people! Female, Annie Weston, thirty-two weeks pregnant plus three, knocked unconscious at the scene of an RTA. Vitals stable. Foetal heartbeat strong, detected in the field and en route. No sign of labour, but we need to assess the injuries, stat.'

Michelle, furious at being sideswiped by both the door and the stranger, sprang up from her position and poked the guy right in the chest. Quite a firm chest, as chests went… Her short, neat little fingernail jabbed into his pectoral flesh, producing a wince from him. He looked down at what was causing the pain as Michelle's team, already called by her, got to work on the pregnant patient and the two casualties in the other rig. His piercing green eyes locked on to her angry baby blues and they sized each other up.

'You almost clipped me with the ambulance door, genius. I don't know who you are, but please step aside.' She gave him a pointed look, turning away to see to her patient.

*Honestly. These mansplainers*, she thought. *They see a few episodes of* Grey's Anatomy *and suddenly they're all McDreamy.*

Although, truth be told, he *was* quite easy on the eye. If you liked arrogant, haughty men with delusions of grandeur. Michelle for one, did not.

The team sped off after the patients, and she went to follow.

'You don't remember me, do you?' came an amused voice from behind her.

She turned, eyeing up the man once more.

'Comobos…a year or so back?'

For a second Michelle just shook her head. Surely she'd remember having seen him before? Or would she? These days she wasn't one hundred percent sure which way was up when she thought of that tour.

Then it came. The wave of nausea, the feeling of being tied to the earth with only a flimsy string, like a helium balloon. One little snip and she would be airborne, helpless.

*Oh, God, not now. Please.*

Michelle felt sick. *Comobos.* That had been the start of it all—of the way she was feeling now. All the emotions that were tied up in that place, that tour, came flooding back.

Looking down at her hands, she saw that she was clasping her hands together tightly, the white gloves she held making her skin look all the paler alongside them. She took out her hand gel and coated her gloves with it, relieved when her hands were still again. Tremors were certain death to surgical careers.

'I was there. I don't remember you, though.'

She didn't elaborate, but waited for him to explain himself.

He smiled easily. 'I had to go wheels down before the end of the tour—left in a bit of a rush.'

His jaw flexed, and she saw something akin to pain flashing across his features. It was only there a moment, and then he put his smug mask back on.

'Rebecca's your close friend there, right? The nurse?'

*Rebecca.* Michelle swayed a little on her feet as a memory of her friend's face, twisted in panic and pain, slapped her. She practically growled at the man, hating him for ruining her first day back. She wanted to be normal; how could she do that with all this around her?

'Yes, she—' *Was.* A simple word, but Michelle couldn't spit it out. 'Rebecca's a friend.'

Then it hit her. This was him. *The* him.

'You're the doctor, aren't you? The one with the crème brûlée?'

The man smiled wolfishly.

Michelle didn't respond.

Rebecca, on that tour, had had a 'friends with benefits' relationship with some flash doctor. They had worked together before, briefly, but she hadn't really registered him at the time. Michelle and Rebecca had nicknamed him Mr Sweet Tooth after he had once managed to produce just the dessert that Rebecca had been craving since arriving in the Army camp, where such things had been almost impossible to get.

She could see Rebecca now, sitting on her cot, laughing with Michelle about her sexploits with him, and the delicious puddings he had provided. It was a nice memory, and one she was glad to remember. Even if *he* was the one to evoke it within her.

'I see my reputation precedes me,' he quipped.

'That *was* a pretty nice dessert. How is dear Becks? Wheels up again?'

Michelle shook her head and he frowned, catching her sudden change in demeanour.

*She's dead.*

'Something like that. Forgive me—I have a trauma centre to run.'

She turned away before he could question her further. She did have work to do, and memories, good or bad, weren't going to save any lives today.

'Sure, I'll see you around,' he called after her.

'Yep,' she said in reply.

*Doubt it, bucko. Relatives' lounge for you, dude. No work for you today.*

Passing Alan, who was pushing a patient in a wheelchair into the foyer of Trauma, she beckoned him closer.

'Alan, we have a family member outside—a doctor. Can you show him to the lounge please? I don't want him wandering around.'

She didn't want him about when she was trying to work; she needed to focus. She put her hands by her sides, nipping at the skin of her thighs to ground herself. She felt better here. If she could see her hand on her scrubs, feel the slight pain her fingers produced, then she was fine. She was here. Safe. Alive and intact—for the most part. Once he was gone and forgotten about, she'd be just fine.

'When you get a minute.' She smiled at Alan, grateful to see him there.

Alan nodded, but then, looking back at the doors, he stopped, his face dropping.

'Er...*that* man?' he checked.

Michelle turned to see Dr Dessert heading over to the pregnant woman. Michelle nodded, groaning. 'Let him check on his loved one— then he goes to the lounge.'

She passed a glance over at them. He was checking the monitors, asking the nurse with the patient questions. She'd let him get some peace of mind, then off he needed to go. She didn't want him hanging around. The thought of him being there thrust the past into her present. She couldn't deal with that today. She was back, and she needed to work.

Alan was looking at her gormlessly.

'Problem, Alan?' she asked.

Alan looked down at the man in the wheelchair, who shrugged back up at him. 'Sorry, pal, I'm just along for the ride.'

Alan sighed, patting the man gently on the shoulder. 'You and me both, brother.'

His meaty hand almost dwarfed the man's whole shoulder, and his dark-tinted skin looked all the deeper against the whites and yellows of the hospital gowns and blankets.

'Michelle, you need to speak to Andrew.'

Andrew Chambers was just asking his secretary to hold all calls so he could have lunch, his hands wrapped around his favourite steak and cheese sub, when the door nearly came off its hinges with a determined knock. He dropped the sandwich in shock, heading to the door, and groaned slightly when he saw who was making her presence felt.

'Michelle, you scared me! What's wrong?'

He picked up his sandwich again, taking a huge bite as his chief of trauma stood before him, her arms folded. His secretary, Rita, came running in on her little heels.

'Sorry, Andrew. I asked her to wait till I could announce her.'

Andrew smiled through his mouthful, waving her away.

'It's fine, Rita,' Michelle replied, increasing

her glare level to singe, her eyes never leaving Andrew's pale blue ones. '*He's* the one who should be apologising.'

He swallowed, wiping his mouth with a paper napkin. 'Rita, you can take your lunch now; get the secretarial pool to field my calls till you get back.'

Rita nodded, taking her leave, and Michelle closed the door behind her, throwing her scrubs-clad body into one of the chairs. She grabbed the other half of Andrew's sandwich.

'Hey! *My* lunch! Michelle—come on!'

She took a huge bite, chewing and devouring it fast. 'Not bad—bit more pickle would have been nice.'

'I hate pickles.'

'I know!' she retorted, dropping the rest of the sandwich back onto his plate. 'I hate a few things too—like coming back to find you've hired some other doctor to take my job!'

Thinking about this job had kept her going all these months since she'd returned to British soil, bringing Rebecca's body with her. After Scott had left, when she hadn't been able to get out of bed… The thought of losing it was making her react, and she couldn't help it. She felt threatened—as if the ground beneath her feet was turning to sand, shifting…

There was a gentle tap on the door, but the pair of them ignored it. Andrew laughed softly—out of awkwardness, probably. Michelle didn't see any humour.

'I had to get some help in because you kept leaving! The trustees of the hospital have ring-fenced some additional funding for Trauma and they want a figurehead. We have all the state-of-the-art machines now, and staff morale is high, but we need more. We need leadership, Michelle. You can't run a trauma centre from the back of a Chinook, as much as you *think* you can.'

The tap on the door came again, and Andrew stood up from his desk.

'You should have discussed this with me,' Michelle insisted. 'I said I would be back, and I am. We both agreed to those deployments. It's a good programme that helps me to sharpen my skills and bring back knowledge to be used here, where we have more facilities. It's a win-win—*your* words! And I did it; now I'm back. I don't need some alpha male peeing all over my territory.'

*And it feels like he's brought the ghost of Rebecca with him, too. I just can't lose this job. Not yet. I just can't lose anything else. I won't be able to handle it.*

'I respect you as a boss, Andrew, but this was the wrong move. I thought we were friends, truth be told. And I'm angry.'

Andrew sighed heavily. 'We *are* friends, Michelle; you're my star employee and you know it. But I need stability. Would you honestly want anything less for this place?'

She wanted to argue, but he had her there. She did want the best for St Marshall's, for her patients. She just wasn't sure how she would feel if that ultimately meant she had to step aside for someone else. Especially *that* someone else.

Andrew went to open the door as the knocking came yet again, casting her a sheepish look on his way back.

'Hello,' he said to his visitor. 'You might as well come in.'

Lo and behold, that man was there again, with the same smug grin on his face.

'The traumas are all stable, head scans all clear. The pregnant woman—Annie—should be waking up shortly. Bang to the head but no permanent damage. Could have been a lot worse.'

Michelle couldn't help but agree with that— at least in her head. She knew they'd all seen far worse happen in much less of an incident. He seemed to know his stuff—not that she'd lower her guard around him any.

'You could have told me she wasn't your loved one down there.'

'Why did you assume that she was?' he fired back easily, leaning against the wall, one foot crossed over the other.

God, he was arrogant. He was wearing an expensive suit, a crisp white shirt, and a tie with swirls of green that brought out the colour of his eyes. His macho, mocking eyes.

'I came out of that ambulance as a doctor— *you* made the assumption. I was on my way in to work when I saw the accident and stopped to help. Made sense to catch a lift with the ambulance. How long are you back for?'

'For good now, actually. No more overseas plans in the pipeline... Andrew?'

Both doctors turned to Andrew, who was

back behind his desk, quietly watching the pair of them as he ate the remainder of his lunch.

'Well, Michelle, that's kind of the problem…' He sat back in his chair, motioning for them both to take a seat. 'This is Jacob Peterson, and he's one of the best trauma surgeons there is, and with you flitting off—'

'"Flitting off"?' She jumped on his words. 'Hardly, Andrew—and *you* gave me permission to deploy with the team, remember? Good publicity and all that?'

Jacob sat down, opening his legs wide and slouching languidly.

She pointed down at him. 'Please, do make yourself and your junk at home.'

Andrew choked on his sandwich a little, but Jacob Peterson just looked at her, a smile dancing across his amused face, making his muscular jaw twitch.

She turned back to Andrew. 'Andrew, just what are you saying?'

Andrew sighed, savouring the last hunk of sandwich before swallowing and addressing the pair of them.

'Like I said, this new funding will make us one of the top two trauma centres in the UK, and I am not about to lose any of it by not having effective leadership. The trustees are concerned and, frankly, I've decided to test a theory. Our new trauma centre will be publicly unveiled in less than three months. I need a crack team to be ready for the challenge, and a new Head of Trauma. You want the job?'

Jacob tutted loudly, and Michelle could feel her cheeks burn red with frustration. They both knew what was coming.

'You want me to apply for a job I already have? I appreciate that cover was needed when I was away, but I'm back now, so surely this isn't necessary?'

'Hey,' Jacob countered. 'Technically, love, the job's mine as much as it is yours.'

She wanted to go with the first response that popped into her head: *Not likely, player. Move along, job-stealer. I need this more than you will ever know.*

Scott had always said that she put the job before anything else. Before him.

*Good job he didn't stick around to see this,* she thought to herself. She was actively hating a stranger now, for daring to exist in the world when so many didn't any more.

'No offence, Jacob, but I hold the position. I know the job and the staff. I'm here, ready to work. I'm sure you have other opportunities to pursue.' Her lip twitched on the word 'pursue'. She knew his usual methods of occupying his time.

*Rebecca told me all about them.*

He laughed—a soft little relaxed sound—and stuck his tongue out at her. Well, he licked his lips, but it felt as if it was aimed at her. She felt a flash of something, but brushed it away in revulsion.

*Down, sweet tooth.*

She looked at her boss, but he was oblivious.

'So that's it?' she demanded of Andrew. 'I go abroad for four months, to help people who really need it, and then I come back and have to fight for my job, against *him*?' She hiked a thumb over her right shoulder at her rival. 'He's probably boffed half the nurses already.'

'The nice-looking half, sure,' Jacob quipped, and there was a challenging look evident in his expression.

Michelle didn't smile, thinking of Rebecca again. *Dear, sweet, funny Rebecca.*

'I'm not worried. I like it here, actually, so I say bring it on. What do you say, Mich?'

She stood up straight, drawing herself up to her full height. She tolerated 'Mich' from people she knew and trusted, but *his* use of it sent a wave of rage charging through her body. He mirrored her actions, straightening his tie. She was five ten—more when she was out of her trainers and in a pair of heels—but she still had to look up at her suave rival.

'What do I say?' she said to both men, her arms folded to keep her from flailing them about like a child in the throes of a tantrum. She'd never give them the satisfaction. She couldn't be childish about this.

So she'd left, and the place hadn't been able to run on its own. They'd needed Jacob. But now she needed her job—her normality—back. She needed him to leave so she could burrow back into her comfortable life. That was her plan, and she didn't have a back-up. No matter what he had meant or hadn't meant to Rebecca, she had to be the victor in this fight. She wasn't sure she would be able to get up again if she got knocked down this time.

'Bring it on. May the best doctor win.'

'In six weeks I'll make my decision about who gets to lead the new trauma centre as head of department,' said Andrew. 'Don't let me down; I need you both at your best.'

'Six weeks of working together...' Jacob smiled, his pearly whites flashing as they caught the light. 'How ever will you resist me, let alone win?'

Michelle looked him up and down pointedly, ignoring the frisson that his sculpted body produced in the pit of her stomach.

'I'll survive, I'm sure.'

She held out her hand, and he shook it, holding it between them. The warmth from his hand pervaded her bare skin.

'We'll see, shall we? This is going to be fun.'

'You really said that?' Nurse Gabby's mouth formed a huge 'O' as she and Michelle waited in the queue at the canteen. It was quiet, being too early in the day for the lunchtime rush. 'I swear, dermatology never gets action like trauma. What did they say?'

Michelle rolled her eyes at her friend, who was reaching over the small child in front of her to get a carton of apple juice. The little girl looked at the juice, and then tried to reach for one of her own.

'They looked a bit like you do,' Michelle quipped, mirroring Gabby's shocked face back at her.

Gabby burst into laughter.

'I don't know…it is what it is. We'll just have to see what happens.'

Turning back to the line, Michelle saw the little girl still struggling and passed her a carton of juice. The girl, dressed in white trousers and an orange flowered top, eyed her warily.

'There you go,' Michelle said, smiling at her and leaning down to meet her eyeline.

'You got any germs?' the little girl asked, her adorable little voice quiet and timid.

'No,' Michelle said, in an effort to comfort her. Pulling out her sanitising gel, she showed it to the girl. 'I use a lot of this to keep my hands clean. You want some?'

The girl didn't move, so Michelle demonstrated with her own hands, then popped the juice onto the girl's tray. She could see a woman over the little girl's shoulder, watching. Must be the mother. The child held her hand out and Michelle popped a tiny blob on her palm.

'Now rub them together,' she said, and the two of them rubbed in unison. 'Better?'

The little girl sniffed her hands and smiled. 'Yes, thank you!'

The woman came to the counter, to pay for the girl's lunch. As Michelle neared the till the little girl waved at her, before turning away and chattering to her mother. Michelle waved back.

'Cute kid,' she said, looking at the two of them laughing over their meal. 'Hope she's not sick.' It often went with the territory around here.

'She's adorable,' Gabby agreed. 'Not for me, though.'

Michelle nodded absently, looking back at the little family. *One day that will be me*, she had thought once, but that was long gone now.

'Nah.' She pulled her gaze back to her friend, handing over her badge to be scanned. 'Me neither. Besides, I already work with a couple of man-children, so I'm all set!'

The two of them were still laughing as they finished eating, and when Michelle looked back, the girl and the woman had gone.

Once Michelle had left Andrew's office and gone back to work, hiding her obvious discomfort and downright anger about the current situation, the two men were alone. The truth was, they both understood why she was angry. Jacob felt the same—though he was still in shock and hadn't found his voice as quickly as she had.

He'd been rather blindsided by the feisty woman who appeared to have taken umbrage against him the second she'd set eyes on him. It wasn't helped by the fact that he'd once bedded her friend, though he knew Rebecca wouldn't have said anything to get her friend so riled; she'd always known the score. Wheels down, they wouldn't be ringing each other.

*What goes on on tour, stays on tour.*

They'd been colleagues first and bedfellows second. It was company—pure and simple.

He thought Michelle didn't seem the type to use dirty tricks, but when things got closer to the wire she might not stay as frostily civil. She didn't seem the type to baulk at a bit of consenting sex between two people either, and they were all adults here. Though some were more adult than others—or it felt that way at times.

He was still feeling rather like a pimply teen who'd been left to look after a baby, but work was his sure thing nowadays. It always delivered, and it paid well. It kept him getting up every morning, even when he didn't quite know where to start with his personal life. And, as hard as trauma was some days, he knew where he stood. It was always there for him—the precision, the speed, the certainty that had to come with saving lives.

On the wards and in the operating rooms Jacob Peterson was steadfast and solid as a rock. Back home, with the boxes and the blank expressions, the silent reproaches for not being there all the time, he felt lost. Overwhelmed. He could run a trauma centre, but when it came to his own affairs he needed time. Security. This job.

'So, that went well,' Andrew said.

Jacob looked at him in confusion. *'Well?'* He raised a dark brow in his boss's direction. 'Define "well".'

Andrew wiped his mouth on his napkin. 'She loves her job, and it's not been easy for her lately...' Andrew looked across at Jacob as his words tailed off. 'It's not been an easy time for both of you, obviously, and I know coming back to work here is an adjustment compared to being out there. I just need the right person for the job. That's what will bring in the money. Investors buy *people*, Jacob, not medicine. They like a face for their money. That's all this is about.'

Jacob clenched his jaw, knowing he couldn't dispute the truth. 'It doesn't make it any easier, though, that's for sure. Are you ready for this?'

He tried to sound playful, slipping back into the cocky, confident persona he used to give him strength when he felt just the opposite. He was half out of the door, trying to quell his panic at the thought of losing his job, when Andrew replied.

'I think I should be the one asking you that. Michelle's not going to give in easily. I did think she might be off for longer, but…'

'It's fine,' Jacob said, leaning against the door frame and looking every inch the cool, calm, and collected bachelor doctor he embodied.

He just needed to keep it together a bit longer, see this through, and then maybe—hopefully—things would work out. Both here *and* at home. Although he was keeping them separate for now—out of convenience rather than by design.

When he'd gone for this job all he'd been concerned about was landing the gig, buying the house, getting on with it and bracing for impact. Now he had to fight again, and the two worlds had to stay separate for a little bit longer than he had planned, until he was chosen to run the new trauma centre. Then he would be able to see through the fog of disgruntled but rather attractive rivals, broken promises, and terrors in the night.

'Like I said when you hired me,' he said, flashing a passing nurse a grin that made her collide with the wall. 'I want to be here, so I'll make it work.'

## CHAPTER TWO

WHEN JACOB HAD SAID it was going to be fun, Michelle hadn't thought he'd meant forced fun, nor that it would start quite so soon. But now she found herself standing there in a posh dress pulled from the back of her wardrobe—her emergency little black dress that she kept dry cleaned in case she was forced to 'network'.

The very word made her shudder, but these days healthcare was a business. You had to get investors to back you, to pay for the riskier treatments and advances, to bankroll the new frontiers of medicine. In trauma, it quite often meant the difference between life and death, and Michelle hated the fact that a person's health—life, even—could be determined by the cost of medication or whether they had the right machine or tool for the job.

But it was that simple. Money talked, and tonight so would she.

She slowly walked into the huge events room

at one of the top hotels in Surrey, which was hosting this fundraiser. Michelle wondered what was going to happen now that alcohol had lubricated the inhabitants of the space. Usually at these things, when the champagne started to flow people loosened up in both tongue and wallet.

She was here to pimp herself out to the elite, to showcase how sexy and cutting-edge trauma medicine was, how dynamic the staff were, and how they were able to network and save lives whilst doing all they could to be cost-effective. Michelle knew she could do all this—she just didn't relish the prospect.

Why would she when she'd been in some operating rooms a lot worse off than theirs, depleted of supplies, equipment, even light? There the safety of a modern, sterile hospital had been hundreds of miles away... When you were saving a life, watching a person fade away before you, you raced the clock—not a spreadsheet or the bottom line.

She wondered what these investors would make of frontline medicine. Would they see it as sexy? As worthy of investment? She doubted it somehow. That kind of work was half a world away. Out of sight, out of mind for many.

*The lucky many*, she added in her head.

She had cradled dying men who would never make the front page but who deserved to. Who deserved a lot more. Her tights bunching up under her dress tonight was something she didn't have the right to moan about.

A waitress paused beside her, her tray laden with flutes of amber liquid, and she reached for one. The waitress, ignorant of her presence, chose that moment to walk away, leaving Michelle without a drink and looking foolish.

'Can I offer you a drink?' a voice asked from over her shoulder.

Andrew Chambers was standing there, two full champagne glasses in his hands. He looked smart, in a midnight-blue suit that highlighted his tall, lean frame. She recognised the tie he wore because she'd bought two of them last Christmas: one for Andrew from the team and one for her ex, Scott.

They'd gone out for a meal once, Scott and her, and Michelle had pulled on that tie a little as they'd walked to his car. He'd dropped a soft kiss onto her lips…

That had been before her work had required a choice, and Scott had become the thing she'd left behind. He'd never understood, and when she'd got back home they'd both known it was already over.

'Not again,' he'd said, looking at her in disbelief. 'You can't be serious. Can't someone else go? You have a life here, Michelle. A life with me. Can't that be enough?'

She'd taken him out to dinner to tell him, hoping against hope that the relaxed atmosphere and the tone of the night would take the edge off her bombshell. It hadn't. And the way he'd looked at her when she'd told him she was leaving again had haunted her for a long time.

They'd barely spoken when she was on tour, and her calls had often not been picked up. He'd taken advantage of her isolation to ghost her, and she'd known he was punishing her for leaving, for choosing work over him yet again. She'd even understood it—had been able to see where he was coming from. She'd already done her bit, sure, but she hadn't been able to make Scott see that a *bit* would never be enough. There would always be battles and people to save.

All she thought about when she was home

was the people she was allowing to die, but she'd never been able to articulate those fears to Scott. Not in a way he had ever come to accept.

After Rebecca, when she'd touched down on home soil, she'd needed him. She'd needed her Scott, her safe harbour. Even if he was never really going to understand what she was going through.

How could he, after all? He worked in an office all day. The calls he made were high stakes, but not life and death. He knew that he would go home every night, safe and sound. That no matter how bad his day at work had been, it would soon be six o'clock. Time to clock off and leave his problems at the door. How could he ever have understood that the woman he loved feared the door every single minute?

They'd gone through the motions of being a couple for a while, but the Scott and Michelle who had fallen in love and moved in together had been no more. Michelle had barely even been a person when she'd got back. He'd stayed for as long as he could, she guessed. That whole time felt like fog to her—a bad dream that had its dark, black roots in reality and had twisted them into something unrecognisable.

She took the flute from Andrew gratefully, drinking the lot straight down.

'Whoa, Mich—it'll be a long night, you know.'

She glared at him as she placed the empty glass back into his still outstretched hand. 'Don't remind me,' she retorted, deadpan.

He grinned a little, nodding his head towards a small crowd that was forming in one corner near the bar. 'Well, your rival is managing just fine. You should try it. Loosen up a little.'

Just as the pair of them looked at Jacob, he looked back from the crowd to them. She turned her head away, catching her reflection in the window and taking in her appearance properly for the first time.

She had her favourite heels on—the black leather ones that made her legs look longer and didn't kill her feet after an hour. They were plain, but elegant, matching her LBD. She had washed her hair, curled it, and allowed it to fall down her back and cascade over her shoulders.

When she looked back at the crowd, as Andrew started making small talk with a person nearby, she locked eyes with Jacob and realised he had been watching her. The thought of him looking at her made her cheeks flush, and she was glad she'd made the effort to look good this evening. Whether or not Jacob had felt the same flip of the tummy as he looked at her as she had on seeing him she couldn't tell, but his face showed that he wasn't entirely indifferent.

She allowed him to look at her for a little longer before he went back to entertaining the crowd. Before she went back to watching him. He was behind the bar now, mixing drinks and sliding them down the bar towards delighted men and women who were whooping and cheering him on, shouting out cocktail orders when he pointed in their direction.

He looked good—even Michelle would concede that point, if only to herself. A beautiful disaster. He was wearing a black tuxedo, his white shirt open at the neck, his black bow tie hanging haphazardly from one of his pockets. Michelle could see a sprinkling of chest hair peeking out from his open collar, and found herself wondering whether there was a happy trail of hair further down, under the layers of his formal attire...

'Good, isn't he? Apparently he's something of a charmer. He seems very much at home being the centre of attention.' Andrew was back by her side now.

Michelle nodded dumbly, her emotions flitting from horny to annoyed to being reluctantly impressed by his antics. He had the whole room in the palm of his hand, and everyone was lapping up his words as he made cocktails even as he discussed the attributes of the new trauma centre and how it would revolutionise trauma care at St Marshall's.

'You awake?' Andrew quipped.

Michelle broke her gaze away to address her boss. 'Sorry, still a little tired, I guess. I should get in there.'

She needed to make her presence felt, so the benefactors knew they had other options beside this Tom Cruise wannabe.

She strode over, placed her clutch on the bar and flicked back her auburn hair. Jacob's eyes flashed as he watched her approach, making them look like emeralds against his thick dark lashes. Giving her a nod that looked like approval, he addressed the crowd. Ever the showman.

'Ah, ladies and gents, we have a treat for you this evening. The very talented trauma surgeon and overseas medical veteran Michelle Forbes. Say hello, Michelle, and tell us what cocktail you'd like.'

He flashed her a broad grin and she smiled right back like a big cat, showing him she had teeth too.

'Thank you, Jacob,' she said confidently, stepping forward as the crowd parted for her and walking right behind the bar.

She looked around her, smiling and greeting everyone as they watched her pass by, her dress swishing.

'Good evening, everyone. I am indeed Dr Michelle Forbes, and I thank you all for taking time out of your busy lives to come and celebrate tonight. As ever, we at St Marshall's aim to be at the forefront of trauma medicine, and our new trauma centre will be second to none.'

She placed her hands on the bar, pointing behind Jacob to a bottle of her favourite whisky.

'My favourite cocktail is pretty obvious, given my background and my favourite drink. Any guesses?'

There was a delighted murmur from the

crowd, and Michelle allowed a little wry smile to play across her lips as she locked eyes with Jacob. He smiled back—a slow, languid smile that made her stomach flip. The man was so good-looking it wasn't fair. He knew how to work a crowd too.

She found herself assessing him with her eyes, up and down, slowly, deliberately, in an obvious way. She felt bold, buoyed up by the hit of champagne and the smell of challenge in the air. The delighted guests around her were giggling away, whispering to each other and shouting out cocktail names like Slippery Nipple and Harvey Wallbanger.

Jacob said nothing, just listened to the people in the crowd building themselves into an excited frenzy around them.

'Nope, no one has guessed it yet,' Michelle said after a while, and then she turned her back to the bar and lifted herself onto the polished metal surface.

The crowd booed, making her laugh. She was just scrabbling to stand without flashing her underwear when she felt a hand on her shoulder. Turning, she saw Jacob, also standing on the bar now, his hand open and outstretched.

She looked at him, trying to decide whether to take it or not, and he winked at her. Her hand felt the coolness of his skin as his fingers wrapped around hers, pulling her to her feet.

Putting his hand momentarily on her hips to steady her, he took the opportunity to lean in and whisper, 'Any clues, Doc? You look amazing, by the way.'

'Really? I think *you* look a little casual,' she said, tapping a finger against the skin exposed by his open collar. 'And you should know I never give anything away I don't want to.'

She took a slight step back, away from him, barely noticeable to anyone else but them. Jacob looked down at their feet and then back up at her, his long lashes making his green eyes look all the more alluring.

'Noted, Doctor.' He spoke in a deep rumble, his voice husky. 'The floor is yours.'

They both stared at each other, and the crowd around them was just white noise. If they had been two strangers in a bar right now would she still be staring dumbly at him? Or would she be lost in the search for that happy trail?

It took everything she had in her to turn away from him, to snap back into the moment.

'So...' she said to the revellers, who were now well into their third, fourth or fifth free drink and thoroughly enjoying the entertainment.

Her body felt as though it was tingling from Jacob's touch, his lingering look, and she had to concentrate hard on what she was meant to be saying. She knitted her fingers together in front of her, keeping them close to her chest.

'Who wants to hear about what we do?'

The crowd, delighted by the showboating doctors, erupted into excited whoops and a chorus of 'Me!'

Jacob looked across at his rival, who was now answering a question about the crash team from one of the bigwigs. She was leaning down, right in his eyeline, and Jacob could see that the man and all those around him were enthralled by her answer.

Whatever the reason for the two of them being thrown together like this, he found himself not totally hating the idea right now.

He turned back to the crowd and got to work.

A glass broke, its shards scattering like tinkling bells across the polished floor. A cheer rose, and there was a chorus of 'Wahey!' and 'Ooh!' as the last of the stragglers left.

Andrew was standing like a bouncer on the steps down to the entrance, collecting business cards and cheek-kisses from the well-oiled grateful guests.

Michelle was at the bar, legs sideways as she sat atop a fancy stool. She had a pink gin in front of her, and the smell of it reminded her of her friend Rebecca once more. The ultimate girly girl, she'd loved the stuff.

A happy memory popped into her head and she smiled as she allowed it to wash over her. The alcohol in her system was numbing her from the sharp pang of pain, and she hoped this would happen more and more, with her grief healing to a more manageable level of mourning.

She was as proactive as ever with her own mental health. At least she was in her own head. They'd offered her counselling, but she felt fine. She knew the cure: *work*. Always had been. St Marshall's was her rehab. Her home.

The staff from the hotel were all busy around her, cleaning up the debris, putting away tables and chairs, collecting glasses to be washed and polished ready for the next big event.

'Well, that went well.'

Michelle turned to see Jacob taking a seat on the stool next to hers.

'I think Andrew will be getting some calls in the morning and some nice fat cheques.'

She nodded at him, reaching forward without thinking and taking a deep glug of her drink, wincing as she remembered the taste.

'Not a gin girl, eh?'

She shook her head. 'Nope, it was given to me—a guest ordered it.'

It had been one of the reps from some big pharmaceutical company she'd never heard of, trying to get her to buy into some wonder of the modern medical world. They came to these events, invited to court the bottom line, as ever. Cheaper, more effective, safer drugs meant more profit, and more turnover for the hospital. The juggernaut of defying death rumbled on, ever threatened by cuts and the fear of private companies getting a foothold.

'You had a good night then?' she said. She raised a freshly plucked brow at him.

He grinned goofily. 'I did my job, that's all.

*You* were a turn-up, though, eh? I swear, once you started talking they all held their breath. You have a knack for this, you know…no matter what happens.'

There it was. A nod to their impending career battle. He was trying to handle her.

'I have a knack for my job because it's already mine, Jacob. I did this job before you came, remember? Why do you want it, anyway? I thought you would be getting itchy feet by now, eager to be off.'

She kept her tone neutral, but it was hard not to feel a little threatened. There were other jobs, sure, but she needed *this* one. He had no ties, no commitments. Maybe he would leave after the centre opened—once he'd lost the job. Then she wouldn't have to work with him at all, having him second-guess her decisions, silently resenting her for winning.

She would miss the banter, though. It seemed they shared a sense of humour and showmanship she hadn't foreseen. Tonight she had actually had fun with him—had a glimpse of what he would be like to work with. The fact that he was a bit of an Adonis was irrelevant.

'I need a job as any person does—to have

a life. And I could say the same to you about itchy feet,' he fired back, walking around to the other side of the bar and pulling out a bottle of beer from one of the glass-fronted fridges. 'You don't seem the type to just stop. No plans for any more airport departures in your near future?'

Twisting the cap off the bottle, he took a long pull, and Michelle had to look away. She didn't trust herself not to space out over his tanned neck and visible chest. She wasn't about to become one of those simpering women— although a cold shower wouldn't go amiss right now... She lost the battle with her brain and her eyes were feasting on him just as he lowered the bottle and made a satisfied 'Ahh...' sound.

'I'm not the type to stop—you're right there,' she said. 'I just choose to stay here now...for a while at least.'

She knew it would be a long while indeed, given how she had been feeling. When he'd uttered the word 'airport' it had sent a shot of icy water down her spine, making her sit up straighter and reach for her glass once more.

'We shall see what happens in six weeks, won't we?'

He nodded slowly, suddenly distracted. Reaching into his inside pocket, he pulled out his mobile phone, frowning as he read the display. He didn't reply, just closed the message.

'Problem?' she asked. 'Not on call, are you?'

He shook his head. 'Nope, not tonight. You?'

She waggled the half-full glass of liquid at him. 'Nope. Which means I get to finish this before I leave. You're not answering that?'

He took another bottle out of the fridge, coming to sit behind her, draining the first one and tossing it into the large bin one of the waiters was pulling out to deal with the recycling.

'No, I don't think I am. Not tonight. It's just a check-in text. It can wait a little longer.'

He nudged her with his elbow, his arm barely touching hers but making its presence known to her senses. She could feel the warmth of it running up her arm. She wondered whether his hands would be cold to the touch, or as warm as the rest of him.

'That other kind of work we do... I need a break. I'm guessing you do too, or else my arrival wouldn't have ruffled you so much. Am I warm?' Another pull on his beer.

Michelle could feel her defensive shields

coming up around her. 'I have no plans to go back as yet.'

'I know that's the party line—you say it whenever anyone at work asks. That the truth?'

He drank slowly from his bottle, his finger-nails working at the gummed paper wrapper on the side of the frosted glass.

She took another sip of her own, playing for time. 'It's *my* truth,' she said finally. 'I need to be at St Marshall's.'

He nodded slowly, still concentrating on pull-ing at the gummed label. A little pile of paper was growing at the side of the bottle.

'I feel a little like that myself,' he murmured. 'I guess we're stuck with each other, then.' He lifted his bottle, now nearly empty and bare of labels. 'To the next six weeks?'

She lifted her glass to meet his and they clinked in silence.

'Comobos was fun compared to tonight and some of our generous benefactors, eh? I met Mrs Pritchett; she's a character.'

Michelle laughed, seeing Jacob's face light up as she joined in with his attempt at breaking the tension. 'You think Mrs Pritchett is bad…? Her husband is worse. He tried to recruit one of the staff nurses to bed bath him last year. He asked me to come along too…to check a couple of moles in sensitive areas.'

Jacob burst into laughter and she realised how tense he'd been before, how peaceful and calm he was now. Maybe he did need to be here, the same as her. A safe harbour in a stormy sea. Could she get on with him for the next six weeks? She still wasn't sure. He was a threat. Without her job, she'd have nothing to steady her.

'Mole-checking is small fry compared to what Mrs Pritchett was suggesting in my ear. I thought she was going to try and drag me off.'

He made a motion as though he was being dragged away, his muscular arms gripping the bar in faux panic.

Michelle played along, grabbing his hands tight in hers. 'Mrs Pritchett, let him go!' she called out teasingly, laughing her head off as he grabbed her and pulled them both off their stools.

He turned, his hands in hers, changing his grip till he was holding both her hands in between them.

'I've got you,' he said, the laughter dying

away as he looked upon her once again. 'I won't let the Pritchetts bring you down.'

He took a step closer and she followed suit. Or her feet did. They didn't even ask her what she wanted them to do—they just gravitated towards him. They stood centimetres apart, arms linked together, laughing. She felt him run his thumb along hers, just once, and resisted the urge to move her fingers, to touch and explore more of him.

'So...' she said, trying to break the silence, to will her body out of this numb stupor.

'So...' he echoed, moving closer again, his body starting to coil around hers as he moved to bridge the gap. 'What now, Michelle? What's the next move?'

As he leaned forward she could see a napkin hanging out of his pocket, curls of writing on it, words written in lipstick. A number, Written in a woman's hand.

She felt herself bristle at the thought and she clenched her jaw, gently removing her hands from his and turning back to the bar. She needed to be one person again—away from him. Her body felt as if it had been magnetised by his, as if the strength of the pull was increasing the closer she got. She couldn't think straight when he was so up close and personal.

Draining the rest of her drink so fast the ice slammed against her front teeth, and then turning on her heel, she yanked the napkin out of his pocket and laid it on the bar. The ring of moisture left by her glass immediately soaked into the paper, making 'Maria' and her number look like finger-painting, not the work of a woman trying to bag a dashing doctor at a swanky booze-filled do.

'My next move is home, to a nice bubble bath and a set of clean sheets. I'm sure you can entertain yourself.'

*That was too close, too stupid. You can't get close to him, Michelle, you're not ready. And him? He's not what you need. Get moving, medic. On your feet, soldier.*

'Hey,' he shouted after her. 'What's with the attitude?'

She didn't answer him, just kept walking towards the door. She wanted to go home and sleep.

'No attitude—just an aversion to walking horn dog egos and a need for some shut-eye.

See you at zero seven hundred hours. Give Maria my regards.'

She heard him chuckle behind her, and cursed herself for feeling secretly thrilled at the sound.

'Michelle?' he called, causing her to almost stumble on her heels.

What *was* it with that man? Why did he make her feel like a newborn giraffe, all clumsy long limbs? She'd lived through bombs, helped people survive. But the thought of a booty call…? It was another sweaty palm moment she couldn't process in her fragile state.

The feel of him had stirred things within her, but she hadn't got where she was by mixing business with pleasure. She needed to keep her head clear, and she wasn't about to be a conquest on someone's trophy wall. Especially not his. Rebecca was on that wall, and she couldn't—wouldn't, shouldn't—forget that.

'Yeah?' she replied, only half turning to look at him over her shoulder.

'Blood and Sand,' he stated, with no hint of a smirk or a simper. 'That's your favourite cocktail. Right?'

She didn't answer. She let the soft swish of the closing doors do that for her.

*Damn.* The man had her pegged better than she'd thought. Blood and Sand *was* her favourite cocktail, bar none. Just her luck to find a man who ticked so many boxes, but stood in the way of everything she wanted and needed.

If Scott were a fly on the wall, he would consider it karma. He'd said the same to her so many times.

The doors swished closed, taking Michelle and her answer with it, but he'd seen the way her shoulders had risen when he'd spoken of her favourite drink. He'd got it right—he knew it. He knew *her.* Or he felt as though he did. Which was weird, given the short amount of time they'd spent together.

*Stop it, Jacob. Think about the job.*

Going back behind the bar, he uncapped another bottle of beer and reached for his phone. Ebony had called him now—at this time. What was going on at home? He would have thought she'd be in bed. He was seeing her in a few short hours, and he was already dreading the inquisition that he knew was coming.

Every time he walked into the place he felt as if he had to account for his whereabouts. It was nice to feel wanted, but this was a little too close for comfort. He didn't enjoy the look of distrust in her eyes, though it was one he guessed he'd earned on occasion. People always said that guilt went with the territory, but this wasn't quite what he'd expected to feel.

He felt drained at the thought, and he pushed his phone into his pocket without calling back. It wouldn't do any good at this time anyway.

He thought of how close he had just been to Michelle, the way she'd allowed him to take her hands, the little gasp she'd made in the back of her throat when he'd brushed his body against hers. She was a puzzle to him, and yet he wanted to know each individual piece, each smooth edge, every jagged facet.

He felt that some of the pieces might fit him too—might solve his puzzle. They were the same in many ways, and it was this that confused him. Did she see through him? Through the bravado? He'd felt they'd begun to bond until she'd seen the phone number in his pocket.

He looked at the wet napkin on the bar. The number was barely visible. He could call her right now—Maria—and have company for the night. For a few nights. A body to hold…someone to wake up to. Usually that was enough, but things were different now. He had to grow up. He had to…

'You about done here?' The manager appeared at his side. 'We're just closing up. Did you get any good leads?'

Jacob stood up, patting the man on the shoulder. 'I did, thanks—plenty of stuff I'm keen to follow up on.'

The manager smiled and said his goodbyes.

As Jacob left the venue, heading for his waiting taxi, his phone buzzed again. A text this time. Another faceless woman from his contacts, with an empty bed and a late-night itch that needed to be scratched.

He opened the reply screen, but after a beat he put the phone back into his pocket and slid onto the black leather seat of the taxi. When asked, he gave the driver his home address.

'Good night?' the affable driver asked. 'Looks like it was a big event.'

A flash of memory popped into his head, making him smile. Michelle, walking the length of the bar, explaining in great and gruesome detail the work they had done that day, detailing their slick operations and their Hail

Mary moments of trauma, the audience watching her intently, the venue lit up by her energy.

'It was, yes—we did well. I'm ready for home now, though.'

The driver caught his eye in the rearview mirror. 'Hot date?' he asked, his smile teetering on the precipice of a leer and evident even in the dim glow of the streetlights.

'Something like that,' he said, thinking of Ebony, who should be fast asleep in bed, not waiting for him to come home. 'My daughter needs a bedtime kiss from her old pops.'

The driver grinned, the leer gone without a trace. He pointed to his console, where a photo of an attractive woman and two small blonde-haired girls sat.

'I can't fault you,' he said, his eyes back on the road. 'Nothing like having a daughter to warm your heart. My wife and I are so happy. You married?'

Jacob looked out of the window to where a couple were sitting on a bench in the street, utterly wrapped up in each other, laughing and joking. It made Jacob's fists curl.

'No, I was engaged once. My daughter's

mother. It didn't work out and she left. The job, I guess. I work a lot.'

The driver flashed him a look of solidarity. 'I get you there, pal. The hours I work, our lass always has her hands full. I'm sorry though, mate, must be tough.'

Jacob didn't answer. Resting his head on the back of the seat, he had already drifted off to sleep.

## CHAPTER THREE

'THIS IS GOING TO HURT.' Michelle gave her patient, a biker with more tattoos than visible skin, an encouraging nod. 'On three, okay?'

She moved closer, setting her feet hard on the floor and holding his dislocated shoulder in position as best she could, whilst avoiding causing the patient further pain by touching his broken ribs. Thank the Lord of Bikers for thick leathers and helmets. One thing that bikers did well was to protect themselves from the hard surface of the road.

She caught a whiff of blood and smoke and inhaled deep. What *was* it about her that liked the smell of danger in the air? Scott had used to say she had gasoline in her veins. But that had been back when he'd thought it cute, and not a relationship deal-breaker.

'One...'

She felt more alive today—being back here, being busy. Her shifts here grounded her, made her forget. Made her feel her usual strong self. She was starting to feel…

'Two…'

*Crack!*

'And three—there we go.'

She helped a nurse to strap up his shoulder, and the relief on the burly biker's face on top of her own assessment told her that the bone was back in the socket. The closed reduction procedure had been effective.

'Good. But no riding for a while, okay? I'll leave you with the nurse, who will get you X-rayed again and then settled on the ward.'

She was just heading to the door when it opened in front of her. She was smacked square in the face by strong male cologne. Woodsy. Familiar.

*That open collar…*

'What've we got?' Jacob asked, looking straight past her to the patient.

She could feel her endorphins decrease just from his presence. Images of last night at the bar kept flicking through her head. She'd dreamt of him last night—of him closing the gap between them further, of his lips… Which would probably still have been warm from the touch of Maria, the napkin chick. Iced water couldn't have stopped *that* train of thought any quicker.

*Snap out of it, Michelle. Work, remember? Routine, normality. That's how this works now. He is the obstacle and you need to get around him, not climb him...*

'*I* was here on time,' she said pointedly, 'and *I* had this patient, who came off his motorbike. Bruising, mild concussion, four broken ribs, dislocated shoulder. Just reset.' She unpinched her face and turned back towards the patient. 'That sound about right, Mr...er...?' She glanced down at her notes again. 'Mr Throttle...'

'Lunch,' Jacob said.

'What?' Michelle asked, looking nervously back at him.

'Lunch. I forgot my lunchbox at home. Had to go back.'

'Right,' Michelle said, pulling a face that made Jacob laugh.

The biker smiled at his doctor as she left.

Jacob still loitered in the doorway.

'Dr Peterson,' Michelle said over her shoulder by way of dismissal, as she left the examination room. She headed to the nurses' station to update the biker's chart and move on to the next patient.

It was a foggy day, which had thrown the inhabitants of Surrey into confused chaos, and accidents were trickling into the trauma centre at a steady rate. Michelle and the staff knew that this would change—for better or for worse. If the fog lifted, the casualties would become minimal. If it worsened, it would bring more confusion and chaos with it. They could feel the crackle of nervous tension and adrenaline as it swirled and filled the air around them.

'Dr Forbes,' said Jacob in a faux professional voice from behind her in the corridor.

She kept walking—fast.

'A moment, please?'

'Are you looking for something in particular?'

Jacob fell into step beside her easily, and she couldn't help but be amused by the squeak of his expensive leather shoes as he strode along, matching her step for step. He looked so relaxed…carefree. If she could have plucked him out of the corridor and put him into a park his easy gait would have fitted in well.

She had never been one for taking dainty little lady steps, even as a teen. She always had somewhere to be and a sense of urgency to get there. Just like now. But now, instead to trying to get somewhere, she was finding herself strolling too…

'Not really—just wondering how you're settling in. I think you'll probably have seen by now that I've made a few changes. I *did* want to tell you last night, Cinderella.'

Was that a clumsy attempt to make conversation, or was he nervous about the alterations he had made while she'd been overseas? The Cinderella barb reminded her of the napkin. She'd always hated the name Maria. Sounded too Von Trapp to her. Too perky.

'The new coffee in the doctors' lounge is terrible.' She frowned at him, pulling a face as they passed the lounge. 'That change wasn't needed or wanted. What else? The new colour-coded filing system? Anyone can stick a few coloured dots around, Jacob. My niece could have done a better job, even before her nap, and she's two.'

The truth was, the changes he'd made were minor, but irritatingly effective.

'Your niece? No kids of your own, then?'

She stopped and glanced at him. He stopped too, a fraction of an inch too close, and held up his hands in surrender.

'Sorry, I know. Inappropriate and personal. I was just asking because we have to work together and I want to find out more about you.'

His stance had changed; his shoulders were hunched over. They were both stationary in the corridor now, facing each other, hands on hips. People were walking around them, the odd rubbernecker showing interest in the intriguing pair.

'Andrew speaks highly of you, and you ran this department for a long time. I just thought that us getting along might be easier than all-out war.'

'Yes, I *did* run this department—and look what thanks I got: I was replaced by an ape.'

She jabbed her finger at him half-heartedly, and his lips twitched in amusement.

'A usurper.'

He pursed his lips and she puffed air out of her own.

'Listen, it's not you, okay? I wasn't expecting this when I got home. I just wanted to get back to work. I have a niece who thinks her aunt is pretty cool. No kids yet—the job, I guess. Never the right time, is it? Don't exactly fit around our hours, do they?'

He nodded, a look of understanding crossing his rugged features. His mouth opened, but he hesitated.

*He gets it*, she thought to herself. *He's been there.*

She pushed the thought away and shrugged at him. 'Better get on.'

He nodded once, closing his mouth, and then stepped to one side as though to let her pass.

'I'll let you go,' he said softly. 'When you have time, I would like to talk, though.'

She dipped her head noncommittally and headed off down the corridor.

Isaac, one of her best nurses, was just finishing up a call when she got to the station and rested her head on the desk.

'Bad morning with Mr Man Candy?' he asked, nodding his perfectly coiffed hair in the direction of Jacob as he headed the other way. Probably to flash his perfect teeth at some unsuspecting female.

'Bad week in general. What do you make of

him and Andrew? He's pitted us against each other for the Head of Trauma job.'

Isaac pulled a sympathetic face. 'You know Andrew—it's all for show. He's just mad that you went on tour again and made his job harder. He'll get over it. He's having a tantrum because he can't have his favourite toy all to himself. This hospital is his project; he likes all the pieces to stay where he puts them.' Isaac smiled and continued. 'Jacob's not bad, really. Bluster mainly, and a dash of arrogance, but his practice is sound. He's a good doctor, Michelle. Just give him a chance, eh? Not everything is as it seems.'

'I will—and I know.'

She opened her mouth to ask what else Isaac knew about him but her beeper sounded.

'Trauma incoming!' she bellowed, everything else cast aside as she ran to receive the ambulance.

She ran the length of the corridor, brushing arms with a solid body as she rounded the corner, her trainers squeaking on the polished floors.

'Time to talk yet?' Jacob quipped, flashing her a wink as he ran alongside her.

The man looked as if he was out for a jog around the block on a lazy Sunday. What had he been doing? Hiding around the corner?

'Where did you come from?'

'I was almost at the canteen doors when I heard the call. What can I say? Instinct took over.'

He zoomed ahead easily, leaving Michelle's side before she could answer back. She picked up her own pace, feeling a burst of adrenaline running through her. She wanted to whoop out loud, but she stopped herself. She wasn't in the desert now.

A porter transporting a wheelchair patient loomed in front of her as she ran, cutting her path off and causing her to swerve in the corridor before catching up with Dr Show-Off and snapping at his heels. They both bounced into the ambulance bay at once, but Michelle managed to get a sly dig of her elbow into his ribs, causing him to crumple theatrically and making her want to laugh.

'What have we got?' they both barked, panting into the face of the stunned ambulance driver as he opened the rig's doors.

'Who's running this?' he countered, looking from Michelle to Jacob and back again.

'I am,' they said in unison.

Michelle felt like verbally slapping down the man standing next to her, showing him *she* still had authority here, but instead she nodded. 'Fine, he's the lead on this one. Run it.'

'Lucas Masterson, aged twelve. Was retrieving a ball from a neighbour's shed roof when he slipped down onto some steel railings. Impaled through the right arm. the steel was dealt with on the scene by fire and rescue, and he was cut down as best they could with the jaws. He's been given ten milligrams of morphine and has remained conscious throughout. Parents were at work, but they're on the way.'

'Thanks.'

Jacob took the lead instantly, walking backwards alongside the gurney as it was gently pushed into the trauma centre.

'Hey, Lucas, I'm Dr Peterson, but you can call me Jacob—or Jake for short. Dr Forbes, here, calls me "idiot" sometimes, so I'll answer to pretty much anything.'

Lucas gave a little smile in response at that,

and Michelle felt her own lips curling in something akin to amusement.

'Football Sunday not going well, eh?' Jacob asked. 'What position do you play?'

Lucas, looking pale and drawn, turned to look at Jacob.

'I'm a goalie,' he said proudly. 'I play for the Jets. We won this morning. I saved a penalty.'

Jacob held up a hand to Lucas's left side and the boy high-fived it.

'Brilliant—we could use you on my team. We suck at the moment.' He made a face at Michelle, who was following at the other side. 'Brighton… Lost my shirt last weekend.'

'Lost your shirt?' Lucas echoed, looking confused. Jacob laughed.

'Yep, I threw it in the bin after the game.'

Lucas gave a laugh too—a little croaky and muted, but there. 'My dad would think that's well funny. We love Spurs.'

In the bay now, Jacob and Michelle pulled one cot-side down each and got to work.

'Spurs!' Jacob squeaked. 'Dr Forbes, we have a Spurs fan here. Watch him closely.'

Lucas giggled, and Michelle's heart clenched. Lucas's colour was returning a little, and she couldn't help but think that it wasn't just down to the pain relief kicking in. Jacob was a natural with the kid. Maybe he had a niece or two of his own tucked away somewhere.

Lucas winced as he tried to move. 'It hurts, Jacob.'

He had gone from brave boy to scared little child in an instant. Michelle found herself wishing his parents were here. Jacob's eyes kept flicking to the entrance, so perhaps she wasn't the only one.

'Right, here's the *not* nice bit,' he said, scrunching his nose up to show he wasn't a fan of what he was about to say. 'Lucas, this piece of railing that went and stuck itself in your arm needs to come out, and it probably has germs on it. Do you understand?'

Lucas nodded warily. 'Will you wait for Mum and Dad to come?'

Jacob nodded without hesitation. 'Yes, of course. We need them to sign some forms anyway, but we can give you a tetanus shot now. That will make sure that any rubbish from the railing won't get into your body. Then, when your parents say it's okay, we will give you some medicine to make you go to sleep, and when you wake up it will be gone and your arm will be all stitched up. Isn't that right, Dr Forbes?'

Michelle found herself nodding, watching the nervous patient relax before her eyes. Jacob had the knack, for sure. This side of him—this paternal side—was a revelation to her. Especially after his hot hands on her hips the night before and his napkin-stuffed pocket. What was in there now? Lollipops and stickers? And why, just when she thought she had a read on the guy, did he do a one-eighty in the other direction? Michelle felt as if her head was spinning.

Despite them being in a bay, she could tell the department was busy today. A nurse pulled the curtains around them, but seconds later they was swept back again by a worried-looking redhead.

'Lucas!'

A woman who had the same eyes as the boy in the bed took one look at her son and went white, but she didn't stop moving. She went straight to his good side, taking his hand and kissing him over and over on his left cheek. He grimaced a bit, pulling back but smiling at the same time. A man followed soon after, his trouser pockets stuffed with screwdrivers and other tools. He looked as white as the woman.

'Jesus, Lucas!' he exclaimed, his voice cracking just a little. 'You okay, buddy?' He went to stand behind the woman, both of them now cradling their son.

'I'm okay. It hurts, but Jacob is going to give me a shot and then fix my arm.'

His mum gave a little relieved sob and hugged him awkwardly to her, careful to avoid his injury. She didn't look at it, Michelle noticed, and nor did the dad. They focused on their son—on his needs, his wellbeing. They didn't talk about blame, or what might have happened. They just sat there, chatting to their son, taking every opportunity they could to kiss him, to touch him. They were looking at him as though he might disappear in front of them.

'Michelle?'

'Yeah?' She snapped back into the room.

Jacob narrowed his eyes, his brows knitted together. 'Sorry, Dr Forbes, I just asked if you might be available to assist me in the OR today?'

He flicked his eyes across to the parents, who were both looking at her hopefully. She turned to face them, hand outstretched. Luckily there was no sign of the shaking today. She could handle this in her sleep.

'Of course—happy to help. Do you want to come to the nurses' station with me, and I'll ask one of the team to go through the forms for you? We need to get Lucas into pre-op shortly—he's in good hands.'

The woman took her hand and shook it hard, gripping it tight while she thanked her breathlessly.

Thirty minutes later Jacob was standing in the scrub room when Michelle walked in, ready for surgery in her blue scrubs.

'Hi,' he said, scrubbing his forearms in a relaxed but determined way.

She was glad the lather hid his corded forearms. He was becoming more and more of a distraction to her, something she yearned to look at for some reason, like a painting—though as she got ever closer her keen eyes couldn't find a flaw, or a brush stroke that didn't quite look right. She needed something—some imperfection that would help her to reject him, to get him out of her head. Her life. Her job.

'You okay working with me?' he asked.

'I'm fine. I said you could run point. I play well in a team, Jacob. I'll survive an operation with you, I'm sure.'

'Well, you've got through worse, right?' His eyes narrowed as he looked across at her, both their hands moving under the water now, preparing. 'I heard about Comobos after my tour ended. Africa was a bad one, but you're still here in one piece.'

Michelle's hands stopped, stilled. Just for a fraction of a second she was lost, and then she was back. Back in control, scrubbing hard around her thumbs, allowing herself to pinch and nip her skin as she went. Every tiny tweak of pain helped focus her mind, helped keep her head in the room.

'What did you hear, exactly?'

*Has he been digging around? He doesn't know about Rebecca, or he wouldn't have mentioned her in such a flippant way.*

She knew that about him now. He wasn't cruel.

He looked away, focusing on his task before speaking in a low tone. 'I heard about what happened. I know you were lucky to make it out of there.'

He was good at understatement, though. 'Lucky' didn't even come into it. Some days she still felt as if she was there and couldn't get out. Maybe she never would—not really. Maybe part of her would never escape the heat and death of that day. But she found herself grateful to be here, and that centred her even more.

She was home and about to operate. Happy days.

'Lucky isn't how I would describe it.'

'I know, but what word would?'

She almost snapped at him, but she knew he spoke the truth. 'You planning on going back?' she asked, finding that she desperately cared what his answer was.

Ready now, they hit the button on the wall and walked into the operating room, where a couple of ready and waiting scrub nurses started to glove and gown them up. They worked in silence till they were standing at the side of Lucas's anaesthetised body, where his arm was uncovered and ready to be operated on.

'Well?' she asked impatiently. 'Are you?'

His surgical mask hid his face now, but his eyes were those same glittering emeralds she couldn't stop staring into. They locked onto hers, and she saw his brow crease.

'Are you worrying about me, Doctor? I have to say, I quite like it…'

They were both working on the arm now, slowly pulling the piece of metal out of the flesh, bit by bit, repairing the arm as they went. If they yanked it out all at once they risked massive bleeding, and Lucas needed his arm. He was a keen goalie, a young boy on the cusp of life. He would need two good arms to go and embrace all the world had to offer.

'Not worried, per se, more curious,' she said. 'Bleeder!'

The word had barely left her lips and Jacob was there, stitching the bleeder up and saving the blood flow to the vein.

'Got it—thanks. My touring days are done now, so don't worry. Whatever happens, you won't be sending me off to the front line.'

His eyes pierced through her. She felt exposed, as though she was the one on the table, open and vulnerable.

'What about you?' he asked.

She had been reaching for a clamp on the instrument tray but she stopped dead. It felt cold in her hands as the nurse passed it to her. She looked around her, just for a second, and knew what her answer was. But to him she gave nothing away, and she was glad she could hide her face behind her mask.

Jacob's hands had never stopped moving. 'We have another bleeder, Doctor. I can't take the rest of the metal out without clamping it off first. You got it? Clamp in three, two…'

She assessed the bleeder and applied the clamp. 'One,' she finished for him. 'Bleeder clamped. Once the railing is out, I'll repair it with a stitch.'

Jacob's eyes flashed at her, the green made all the more vibrant by the lights around them. She couldn't be sure, but she thought he was smiling behind that mask. She pouted behind hers, and they each put a hand on the piece of metal. Their fingers brushed against each other's as they counted to three once more.

After that, they were like two parts of the same machine. They worked in unison, their shorthand and skills at speed and under pressure driving them on. He was good—every bit as good as she was, even. He anticipated her moves as she did his; his hands felt like extensions of her own.

'You see this?'

She heard one of the scrub nurses whispering to the other.

'Have they worked together before?'

The other shook her head, her eyebrows high in surprise, and Michelle looked to see if Jacob had heard. He gave her a sexy raised brow.

*Yep, he heard. Geez.*

'Nope, never before. Weird, eh?'

Jacob made an odd noise from his throat—a laugh disguised as a cough. She tried to give him her best angry stare, but that just made him 'cough' even louder.

'Ah, Lucas,' he said to the boy on the table. 'We are having a day, aren't we?' His eyes crinkling at the corners, he grinned unmistakably at all the ladies in the room.

*Ever the charmer,* she thought to herself.

'Come on—let's get this young man back defending that net.'

'The answer's no,' she said softly, after some more time had passed and they had finished closing him up.

Blood flow was looking good, the arm had

pinkened up already, and all his muscles and reflexes were intact. Lucas was a lucky boy.

'No more tours for me either.'

She thought about mentioning Becks, but the thought of speaking about her to him just felt too strange. It reminded her of his past, with Becks and probably countless other women. It confused her already jumbled feelings about him. She couldn't bring those worlds together— not yet. It was all right for him—his world was one big party.

She could feel the adrenaline and excitement of the operation ebb away, leaving her feeling shaky, worn out.

'Your choice, or the therapist's?' he asked.

They were alone now. The scrub nurses had gone off to get more ORs ready, and Lucas was being wheeled into Recovery. They were back in the scrub room, at the sinks.

'I didn't have therapy. Didn't need it.'

Jacob gave her a sideways glance that lasted far longer than was comfortable.

'You're joking, right? Nothing? Not even here? Did Andrew sign off on that?'

*Andrew doesn't know the half of it.*

'Of course he did. It was a tour that ended

badly—that's it. It's happened before and will happen again. I'm back, safe and well.'

*Well, I'm pretty sure I'm taped together well enough. I get by. My work is still the same.*

She kept her hands out of sight as best she could, till the shaking had stopped. As soon as they had finished operating, it had come back. The sick, shaky feeling of being out of control.

She clenched her hands and forced herself to pull herself together once more. When she unclenched, her hands were as steady as a rock.

*What?* Jacob couldn't believe his ears. Andrew had let her come back to work, fight for her own job, without not checking that her head was even in the game.

He'd heard about Comobos, all right—everyone had. The details were sketchy in places, but he knew it had been bad. They'd lost people—a lot of people. Michelle had made it home, sure, but how much of her had actually boarded that plane?

He already knew his previous tour had been his last. Even without his home situation changing he would have been done anyway. The call from home had just speeded things up. There were only so many times you could cheat death before the rules changed and it took you anyway.

He found himself at Michelle's side before he even knew what he was doing. His hands newly clean, he went to touch her shoulder, but stopped himself.

'Michelle, I saw you in there…in the OR. With the clamp. I *see* you. And I know what you're going through.'

'So?' She looked at him blankly. 'You've been on tours; you know how bad it is. I'm fine. I'm working, eating, sleeping—the lot. The clamp was a one-off.' Holding out her hands to demonstrate, she looked everywhere but at him. 'Steady.'

'No nightmares? No sign of anything bad?' He was in full doctor mode now, peering at her closely as though he wanted to strip her down and do a full examination.

'No, Dr Peterson, no scary monsters under my bed. We help the people who kill the monsters, remember?'

She'd switched it off, he realised. Like a light going out. She'd turned off her humanity—

turned herself into a walking, talking, functional doctor-bot.

It was a setting he'd defaulted to a lot over the years, till he hadn't known how to function any more. Till Ebony had come into his life, smashing it apart. Even then, with a daughter at home, he'd still done the tours, the hard stuff. And then Ebony had become the hard stuff, and then he'd stopped. For her. For them both, he realised now.

'I was supposed to join that tour not long after you went out there. I didn't know who had gone—just that they wanted extra bodies.'

She snorted darkly, and he winced at his choice of words.

'The point is, Michelle, I didn't go. I wasn't there that day, so I will never fully understand.' He touched her shoulder now, turning her towards him as she finished drying her hands. 'I *do*, however, have experience of a lot of other bad days, and I know how it feels to come home and feel guilty because others didn't. I get it. But I didn't get through it alone.'

It was on the tip of his tongue to tell her about his counselling, about the fact that his daughter had saved him just by needing him home.

He wanted to tell her about his daughter. About how his heart, beaten and battered in his chest, could hear Michelle's broken heart calling to him like a voice in the dark. How confused he was now that she was here.

She might take his job, affect his life—*their* lives—and he couldn't allow that. How could he make her see that he had pain too? Pain that ran like a ribbon through him, as it did her?

He couldn't tell her about his child.

She stepped a tiny bit closer, leaning infinitesimally towards him. He held his breath and waited for her to make a move.

*If she kisses me I won't be able to stop myself from grabbing her and kissing her back. I need to.*

'Jacob, I'm fine.'

She patted his cheek with an open hand, like a grandmother would. His ego and his hopes deflated like a balloon.

'Better get on. Give my love to Lucas.'

She walked by him, through the doors with a swish. He could still feel her touch on his cheek, and he rubbed at the area. He didn't know exactly what her deal was, but he *did* know a few things.

One, he wanted her so badly his skin prickled when her name was mentioned. Two, she wasn't fine but she was trying to be. And three, when it came to the crunch—her or the job,—he didn't have a clue which one he would fight for and which one he could bear to live without.

# CHAPTER FOUR

MICHELLE STAYED INFORMED on the Lucas case from afar for a little while, getting the nursing staff to provide her with discreet updates on Jacob and his work.

The whole day had spiralled into a day of seeing Jacob's face everywhere and never having a minute to herself. Every minute meant a new case, a new patient, a new decision. The poor nurses didn't know where to put themselves as the day wore on and the workload became tougher.

Jacob was every bit a machine, as she was, and between them they managed all the work together, challenging each other, coming up with surgical plans, the shorthand between them soon becoming familiar to each other.

Just as they had in the OR, they'd developed a pattern of knowing each other's moves. Several times, the two of them had actively disagreed, warring with each other on points of medicine and treatment, but they always to put the patients first.

It was eight p.m. now, and Michelle could feel every second of her twelve-hour shift taking its toll on her still healing body. She did the hand-over, from which Jacob was conveniently missing for the first millisecond all day. Then she waved Isaac and the rest of the outgoing team off, pressing a bunch of banknotes into Isaac's hand as he left.

'For today. Buy yourselves a drink each—at least. Tell Bill I said hello, and to put Lucas on the board for tonight.'

Bill ran The Pub on the Corner—a local public house with a genius name. It *was* on the corner, and only a couple of streets away from St Marshall's, so it was often filled with hospital staff having a pint to take the edge off, or a few shots to celebrate saving a patient—pulling off the cheating of death for another broken and now mending body.

The board on the back wall was for the good ones. A photo or just a name was all that was needed—a chicken scratch on the wall to mark them. The ones the doctors and nurses wanted to remember.

Seeing Lucas settled in bed tonight, his parents watching over him as he slept, was a *good* memory. One to add to the board for sure. He would be a goalie again, with full hand and arm function, and he'd have a piece of metal and an impressive scar to show his teammates.

The fact that it was the first time she had operated with Jacob had nothing to do with her happiness. It was purely about the save.

Isaac went to give her the money back, protesting that there was no need, but she was steadfast in her decision. She closed her hands around his and pressed firmly.

'Don't forget Lucas,' she said, and pushed a photograph of Lucas saving a goal into his hand. His mother had had it in her purse, and had been only too happy to give it to the doctors who had saved her son's arm.

Michelle wanted to promise Isaac and the others that tomorrow would be better, that *she* would be better, but she kept quiet. She knew she'd not been at her best today. She'd been being standoffish with everyone, keeping them at a good arm's length. But she couldn't risk them asking questions she didn't want to answer or noticing how changed she was in herself.

Her teeth set. Scott had noticed—had seen how different the woman in his life had become, how angry and shut off. He'd left, and she didn't want that again. Her colleagues wouldn't understand, so she kept it hidden.

'No excuses—I insist. You all earned it.'

She leaned in closer, touching Isaac's arm in gratitude. She appreciated the loyalty of her close friend, both professionally and personally.

'Well, if you *insist*, boss, I think I can twist a few arms into a bevvy or two.'

She wished him a good night, and he headed to the hospital doors to meet the rest of the tired workers. They all whooped and cheered when he fanned himself theatrically with the wad of notes.

'Drinks are on her!'

He pointed over his shoulder at Michelle, and she plastered a fake smile on her face and raised a hand in their direction. Feeling a little less guilty for her behaviour, she signed off the last few remaining charts and headed to the on-call room. She was on beeper rota for tonight, which was what they called 'on call' around here.

'On call' didn't really translate to working in a battle zone. There was no real rest there; you were always ready for the call, primed for action at a moment's notice. She didn't even change into nightwear at home any more—if she went home. She felt less anxious if she went to sleep ready to jump up in a split second.

After today, she couldn't summon the energy to go back to her empty flat just to stare at the boxes of trinkets and the pictures she hadn't got around to hanging up. Those empty walls mocked her whenever she walked in the door.

Isaac and some of the others had offered to help her move in all those months ago, when she and Scott had started to divide their lives, but she'd refused. Scott had had a flat-share organised already, with his brother, and she had thought that a new flat—a place that only she had lived in—would help her to nest.

But that hadn't quite happened either. She was still waiting to find out where she belonged. Still longing for somewhere to call home, a sanctuary from the days of battling death and disease.

She felt wretched, with a bone-deep lethargy that made her muscles ache and her head swim. She just wanted to get her head down for a while, switch off the world and rest.

'I know, darling, I know. It's not for ever, though, remember? I just need to prove myself in my new job, then we'll have more time. Please, just try. For me…'

Jacob's voice was coming from the on-call room, where the door stood slightly ajar. He sounded different. Softer. Less confident.

'I know, but I'll see you tomorrow. I promise. I love you.'

Michelle balked at his words. This guy had managed to fall in *love*? Everything she had seen and heard of him so far ran contrary to this little love chat. Including his smouldering looks and the way his fingers twitched when she was nearby—as though he couldn't help himself and *had* to touch her. *Especially* his smouldering looks, she thought, as a flash of the green beauty of his eyes behind a surgical mask swam into her memory.

She found herself wondering who was at the

other end of the line, being consoled by him now. What sort of person adored a man like this?

*A person like me.*

She didn't hear anything else, so she opened the door and closed it behind her, feigning surprise at seeing him standing there. His mobile phone was still in his lowered hand.

'Oh, sorry. I—'

'It's fine,' he replied quickly, shrugging her off and turning to one of the beds.

The room was essentially a small square, with a single bed at the left and right of the space, against the walls and facing the door. There was a bathroom off to the right. In the middle, on the far wall, there was a large window, showing the city outside the hospital lit up by streetlights and traffic. They twinkled in the night and she watched them absently.

'I was going to sleep anyway,' he said. He put his phone on charge, taking off his doctor's coat and his shirt before she could make sense of what her tired eyes were feasting on. He wore a white vest underneath. Very John McClane.

'You're staying here?' she asked, seeing her hopes for a few hours of peaceful sleep being dashed before her. Not very *yippee-ki-yay* of him. 'I'm on call, so there's no need for both of us to be here. I'm taking one for the team.'

*Plus, it sounds like you have someone to get home to.*

She took off her own doctor's coat and laid it on the bottom of the bed, shucking her trainers off and sticking them under the frame.

He didn't make a move, and she looked up at him pointedly. 'You've not moved.'

He looked down at her, before sitting down on the other bed and sliding off his posh squeakers. 'You don't need to take one for the team. I kind of thought we *were* the team, after Lucas today. I thought I was on the rota, so I planned to be here. You can go, if you like—get some rest, acclimatise. Word is you have a new pad to settle into. Shouldn't you be shopping for knick-knacks or fluffy cushions or something?'

*I think you'll find the word is 'ugh'.* 'Acting head,' she said.

'What did you just say?' he asked, his eyes looking almost shark-like in the darkly lit room as he leaned infinitesimally closer.

She leaned in closer herself, till their knees were almost touching. She could feel a trace of heat from his body, and felt herself shudder in response. *Why* did she flop into a puddle of goo whenever he was near her?

She swallowed and locked eyes with her rival. 'Acting head—which is what you are.' It sounded weak, even to her, but she was trying to stand firm against him.

'What we *both* are, if you think of Andrew's plan. We're both auditioning for the job. I am on the on-call rota tonight, and I can't swap to another, so you can go home tonight, good Dr Forbes.'

'Fine,' she said. 'But the same goes for me, so you're stuck sharing.'

Jacob's eyes flicked from her face to the bed behind her. She knew he'd see the scrub cap sticking out of her white coat pocket, and that he might remember that he had seen it before, somewhere. She followed his gaze and folded her coat over, hiding the contents of her pocket.

'I'm going to turn in.'

She searched his features for any kind of re-action, but he was all business. She turned on her side, making her green khaki vest top ride up a little as she twisted her body to lie facing the wall. She pulled her lab coat up with her feet and wrapped her arm around it like a child would a security blanket.

She could hear Jacob shuffling about for a while, getting comfy, and then she lay there looking at the wall, listening to his breathing. When it became shallow, indicating that he was asleep, she reached into her coat pocket. Pulling out the scrub cap, she ran her fingernail along its stitching, thinking of her friend and settling her head down onto the soft pillow.

She remembered the day Rebecca had come running up to her from the village, eager to show off her purchases. She'd spent the day at one of the local clinics that had been offering drop-in appointments for healthcare: trauma injuries, dietary problems, vaccinations. They'd treated people as best they could there, offering them the basics that people back home wouldn't even think twice about. Tampons. Fresh water…

Rebecca had loved those days—had adored helping people, feeling useful. It had been one of the things about her that had made Michelle persuade her to come on that last tour with her. Scott had barely been speaking to her for signing up again, and she'd wanted her happy-go-lucky single friend there to make the trip better, more fun. They always had such a good time working together.

'Free Prick and Period Day was a success!' she'd screeched, barrelling into camp and leap-frogging over Smithy, who had been bent double, cleaning his boots. 'We rocked!'

'Becks, knock it off!' he'd said grumpily, but she'd just stuck her tongue out at him and kept running towards Michelle.

'You need to stop calling it that—especially so loudly!' Michelle, ever the professional, had chided her. But that stern talk had lasted all of two minutes, and then she'd been cracking up with Becks about her day and her stories of the patients they'd helped.

'I got this too—bought it from the market.' She'd pulled a small bundle of orange fabric out of her backpack, presenting it to her friend with a devilish glint in her eye. 'We are going to be the best-accessorised medical team this side of the border!'

Michelle felt a tear slip down her cheek as she remembered that day. The easy smile of her friend, the hope and the sheer joy she had put out there every single day, almost to the point of being annoying.

She'd always joked with Rebecca's mum, Kathryn, that her daughter hadn't been conceived—she'd been dropped off at the front door by a unicorn. Kathryn had reminded her of that at the funeral.

She tried to push the thought away, but other memories kept coming. Becks screaming at her to move. Smithy prone on the ground, his boots discarded on the sandy grit nearby. People running from all directions. The acrid smell of burning trucks mingled with the melting rubber of the tyres, the smell of flesh being seared off the bone in the heat...

'Becks!' she'd screamed, grabbing an abandoned gun and running for cover, searching for her friend in the chaos and panic.

The air had been thick with movement and death but she'd kept on pumping her arms and legs, desperate to evade the insurgents hot on their heels.

'Becks!'

She'd heard a voice behind her and, whirling around, she'd seen her. The orange cap had still been tied to her belt, where she'd always kept it. She remembered feeling comforted, seeing it. If they had their talisman caps they were both good…

'Nooooo!'

'Michelle?'

'Becks, no! Stand down!'

'Michelle!'

'You're not supposed to be here! Becks, I'm sorry!'

'Michelle! It's okay. I'm here… I'm here.'

Michelle was in a blind fury. She couldn't find Rebecca, but she could hear her. She was heading towards her voice when a bulky form stopped her. She felt strong arms encircle her, felt her head being pulled back. This was it. This was the time.

Fight, girl—now!

She brought back her head till it touched the tops of her shoulders and then thrust it forward with as much force as she could muster. A primal scream of pain and terror was ripped from her, taking her breath with it.

'Arrrgghhhh!'

The grip on her loosened, disappeared, and she took the opportunity to run. She got to her feet, banged into something. Her legs…she had to run…run and—

She was at the door of the on-call room, her hand on the doorknob, when she came to. The door before her was made of solid wood. There was no chaos. No death. No Becks.

She tried to release the door handle and realised that her hand was gripping on to it for dear life, her knuckles white and stretched taut to the point of pain.

A muffled sound came from behind her, and she turned, pale-faced, to look at the source. Jacob was sitting on the floor, his legs out in front of him, his hands covering his nose. He reached for a pillow from one of the beds, pulling the cover off awkwardly with one hand, his eyes never leaving her.

'Are you back?' he asked softly. 'Do you know where you are?'

She caught a glimpse of the pillowcase, a handprint of fresh red blood, and started to shake. 'Did I—?'

He folded up the pillowcase and pressed it against his nose, slowly standing up. He made no move to come closer, and she was grateful for that. She still felt as if she was standing there, in front of Becks. She looked down at her feet, registering that she was standing on a carpeted floor.

Her shaking hand reached down and started to pinch the skin on her thigh. *Pinch.* Safe. *Pinch.* Alive. *Pinch.* Out.

The shaking lessened a little, and she turned and left the room.

Jacob watched her leave, saying nothing. Once the door had clicked closed he lifted himself off the floor, sitting down on the bed. His nose was broken—he knew that. He'd felt the bone break when her head had connected with his. It wasn't the first time he had been headbutted, but it was the first time a woman had been the perpetrator.

He'd heard her shout 'Becks!' in her sleep, seen her thrashing, and one look at her had told him that she wasn't there. Michelle hadn't been in that on-call room—not really. She'd been standing in a war zone, unaware that she had got out.

Who was Becks? Was it a nickname for a soldier she'd met?

He felt his fists clench at the thought of her

pining for a man. A man who was obviously still on her mind in some way, good or bad. Was it the guy she'd lived with before? He knew there'd been someone because the nurses chattered in their down time.

He caught sight of himself in the mirror on the wall and winced.

'Well...' he said out loud to himself.

Pulling away the pillowcase, he noted that the bleeding had slowed down a little, but he'd still need to get his nose checked.

'This will take some explaining. Ebony is going to *freak*.'

He went to stand, and the door flew open again. Michelle with an armful of supplies. She stopped dead when she saw him there, the pillowcase growing redder and redder by the moment.

'I'm sorry... I can ask someone else to do this if you'd prefer.'

She was standing in the doorway of the still-dark on-call room, the lights behind her illuminating her form. She was biting at her lip, her eyes full of remorse, confusion and concern. She had never looked more beautiful to him.

It took all he had not to walk over to her and

make her forget every moment of the past hour with his lips.

He motioned with his free hand for her to close the door. 'Mich…come in.'

She hesitated a moment, and then kicked the door shut behind her. She knelt by him, gloved hands working fast to get everything ready. Then she shuffled along the floor, positioning her body between his legs, and slowly took hold of the hand holding the fabric. She put the stained cloth into a plastic bag, and winced.

'It's broken…but the cut on top isn't too bad. I can dress it. Are you ready?'

She was already holding his nose, her warm fingertips slightly shaky till the moment they touched his skin. Then she was as steady as they came. Professional Michelle mode.

He nodded—the merest hint of agreement— and she had the cut dressed in mere seconds.

Jacob let her work. The truth was, he was in shock. Not at the headbutt. Hell, people had done worse to him before. At least she had spared the family jewels. The radiology nurse he had gone out with last year hadn't been so generous.

That wasn't it. That wasn't what made his

heart beat faster, made his own memories and panic zing to the surface.

It was the lack of control, the fear—the sheer terror she had showed him in that room.

She wasn't well. And her brand of sickness didn't just go away. It didn't fade with time, and it didn't leave the sufferer with a moment's peace. She was in hell, and he had been her enemy back in that moment.

She wouldn't have stopped fighting if she hadn't come to, if her instincts for survival hadn't kicked in. How could he help her? Did he even want to? This was her Achilles' Heel. If he cut her down at the ankles the job would be his. His position would be safe. And he *needed* this job. He needed to be here—now more than ever. He had a child to raise, and that didn't come cheap.

If she were a man, would he even still be here right now? He'd already be in Andrew's office, ratting his rival out and taking the crown. So what was stopping him? The fact that she was suffering? That her suffering was something he wore too, like a favourite shirt he just couldn't get rid of? Was that it? Or was it because he wanted to know her better?

Right now, with her tending to him, it was hard for Jacob to know which part of his body was currently in control of his decision-making.

'That feel okay?'

She was staring at him now, her auburn hair hanging over one blue eye as she worked. He could smell her perfume, a light sweet scent that lingered in the short space between them. All traces of her panicked state were gone, aside from the fact that her skin was pale and drawn. She was in medic mode, and her hands were as sure and strong as ever.

She didn't look him square in the eyes, but he couldn't stop looking at her. His eyes were processing everything before him, trying to piece the puzzle of her together.

'Jacob, does that feel okay?'

He realised he hadn't answered her, but he wanted to ask so many questions of his own.

'It's good, thanks.'

'I've Steri-Stripped the cut, the wound is clean, and the break will heal itself. You might want to get an X-ray, just in case.'

He nodded slowly, both of them knowing full well that she didn't need to tell him any of this. It was basic training for them—a quick job. She was trying to fill the silence, but for whom he couldn't be sure.

She busied herself tidying away the kit she'd laid out on the mattress. He reached for her hand before his nerve-endings even registered the movement. He slipped his fingers under hers, trapping them lightly and running his thumb along the back of her hand.

She flinched, still sitting between his legs, pinned by their linked arms.

'What can I do?' he asked simply.

When he'd come back from a tour that had been all he'd wanted someone to ask, but no one ever had. The stigma of poor mental health and the Alpha male tradition of manhood still lingered, silencing many in the throes of PTSD. He'd learnt the hard way just how many people suffered under the spectre of anxiety and depression. He'd been lucky to get out before his had got bad. His girl had saved him.

Now he was trying to help Michelle, but she kept taking his breath away, clouding the goal. 'Michelle, if you tell me what I can do, I'll do it.'

She pulled her hand away, slowly gathering the rest of the kit and moving to stand. Jacob stood with her, and as they looked at each other again Jacob saw that she was crying.

All thoughts of weakness disappeared and he took a step forward, encircling her with his arms. She made no move to stop him, but he felt her whole body tense, muscles and sinew turning to cold, hard steel in his embrace.

'Michelle, you don't have to do this alone.'

He had said the same thing to someone else only a short time ago, and he'd meant those words then too. Not that it had done any good. It had to be different this time; he had to work harder. Be better, do more. Fix things. Be there.

'I'm here for you.'

Another crying face popped into his head, and his heart squeezed for them both.

She sobbed then—just one short outlet for her pain before she locked it away again. He could feel her starting to pull away, so he released her, not wanting to push. Her cheek brushed against his, the salty silent tears rubbing off onto his stubbly cheek.

It made his whole body stir into life, and he felt a pang of guilt and confusion.

*You need to tell her.*

## CHAPTER FIVE

THE WORDS HE was whispering in her ear should have soothed her, but the situation was all wrong. He couldn't help her; no one could. Just as no one had been able to help Becks, or Smithy, or any of the other people she had tried and failed to save.

Sometimes life was just dark and broken and people suffered. She got that now.

She started to pull away from him and he let her go without pushing. It wasn't till she saw his face that she realised what was going on. Her whole body felt as if it was tingling; the thought of him being so close was lighting her up from the inside. He felt so good, so comforting, so warm.

She locked eyes with him and saw the same confused need on his face that she felt in the pit of her own stomach. Frowning, she dropped her kit onto the floor and, reaching forward, placed her left hand on his cheek. Leaning in, she dropped a kiss on his lips.

She had barely touched him when she felt him move closer, taking her face in his own hands and tilting his head to deepen the gentle exploration of her lips. She let him, moving in once more slowly, gently, taking care to protect his injury. The injury *she* had caused.

He should have complained, but he hadn't, and she wondered just who *was* this man kissing her so passionately. He moaned, just a little, against her mouth, and her stomach flipped in response. She kissed him back, letting her tongue flick out to massage his, and felt him respond, pulling her down to the bed, wrapping her legs around his waist to hold her in place.

'This isn't a good idea,' he said.

She nodded against his mouth, kissing him back even as he dived back in.

'We shouldn't. We need to talk,' he said.

She felt him run his hands down her back before settling at the base of her spine, pulling her closer to him. She could feel the evidence of his attraction against her body, and he didn't try to hide it from her.

'Stop, then,' she said, running her hands

through his thick black hair, giving it a playful pull that made him growl.

He stopped kissing her, pulling away and searching her face.

'Stop?' he checked, moving his hands away from her bottom to his own hips.

The loss of his lips and touch felt like having a comfort blanket ripped from her, but the cold realisation helped. She looked at his face, at his broken nose, his beautiful dark-lashed eyes, the already developing bruises beneath them, and she was lost to the moment.

She was so sorry—for him, for Becks, for everything—and only his touch numbed the pain.

She lowered her lips to brush them against his once more.

'Dr Forbes?'

Her name was being called through the door, and there was a strong knock against the wood.

'Andrew,' she whispered, her lips so close to his that she tapped the word out on his skin, like Morse code for lovers. 'It's Andrew.'

Jacob's face registered annoyance, but he made no move to release her.

'I'm here—getting changed. What's up?' she shouted towards the door.

Her pager was silent. What did he want?

They both sat there in the dimly lit room, holding their breath, their arms still wrapped around each other.

'The door's not locked,' she whispered into Jacob's ear.

He nodded and lifted her off him. 'You go. I'll come out after.'

'Turn around,' she whispered, and he did as she asked.

She grabbed a pair of fresh scrubs from the pile kept under the bed and changed quickly. She gathered her things and then, waiting till Jacob was behind the door, stepped out, closing the door firmly behind her.

Andrew looked behind her, trying to see into the room.

'One of the A&E nurses has crashed out in there,' she told him smoothly, cutting off his question and holding up the used kit. 'Bit of an accident—all good now. Had to change.'

Andrew's all-seeing eyes landed on the bloodied pillowcase in the plastic bag. 'Nice. Report filed yet?'

*Shit. Andrew never could let anything go. Excellent management skills, but a pain when you were trying your best to dig your way out of a hole.*

'None needed. It was a minor thing.'

Andrew shook his head. 'Still need a report on my desk.'

She nodded, knowing it was impossible to argue. Since there *was* no nurse, she'd just have to hope he wouldn't follow it up later. For now, she needed to keep him busy, and away from the door.

The thought of Jacob in there, hiding, made her head spin. She'd been kissing him, straddling him, touching him.

The man who could take away her job, her career here. The same man she had hurt whilst in the throes of a flashback so vivid that she could still feel the dust and sweat on her skin. The man who had slept with her best friend. The man she was supposed to hate for trying to take her job, for being the type of man she had avoided her whole life—a player. And now he was a player with dirt on her that could cost her everything.

If she lost this job, she would be adrift.

'Did you want something?' she asked, walking away from the door towards Andrew's office.

Andrew fell into step beside her, rubbing the back of his neck. A sure sign he was about to say something awkward.

'I actually wanted to talk to you about the job. I feel as though things have been a little difficult since you got back and I just wanted to check in.'

A nurse sidled up to Andrew, holding a pen and clipboard. He took it from her, read through the notes and signed it with a flourish.

'Do you mean *things* have been difficult or *I* have been difficult?'

*Don't bite, Michelle, you're being paranoid.*

He hushed her, waiting till they were outside his office door, then leading her inside and answering her question.

'I didn't think I handled your return as well as I could have. I know you've made a lot of adjustments already, coming back to work.'

She smiled at her superior, not wanting to give anything away, and not wanting to talk either. 'It's fine, honestly. I—'

An insistent knock came on the door.

'Come in,' Andrew called. 'Sorry, won't take a minute.'

Jacob peeked in, most of his face obscured by a patient file.

'Sorry, boss, Dr Forbes is needed urgently on the floor.'

Michelle grabbed her beeper. 'But my pager di—'

'Network problem,' Jacob said smoothly. 'All fixed now. We need to go.'

Michelle opened the door and Jacob ducked out of sight, leaving the file flapping in his wake. Squeezing through, she shouted, 'Thanks, Andrew,' and half ran after the retreating file.

They walked deeper into the hospital and headed for the trauma bays. Jacob released the file, first checking down the corridor as though Andrew was hot on their heels.

'Thanks.' It was all she could think to say. 'Where's the patient?'

He turned to face her in the corridor, pointing at his nose and now even more black eyes.

'It's me. I think I need that X-ray now. You caved half my face in with your head.'

He crossed his eyes comically, making her laugh.

'The X-ray department is down on the first floor. Plenty of staff on.'

'Ah…' he mused, moving out of the way of a crash cart rolling towards A&E. 'If I speak to them, though, they'll need an explanation. Of how I came to break my nose, on shift, with no witnesses.'

Michelle pursed her lips. 'I *am* sorry—I didn't mean to. You surprised me. I feel awful.'

'Is that why Andrew was talking to you back there?'

*What do I say? Yes? Mind your own business?*

'No. I didn't tell him about your nose. I would have had to explain what happened.'

The penny dropped and realisation set in. Passing by a supply cupboard, she came to a halt, moved away from the people walking past.

'That's it, isn't it? You're going to tell him so you get the job.' She leaned against the wall, her head resting on the painted surface as she looked up at the strip lighting. 'I assaulted you, I'll have to resign, you get my job by default.'

'What?' His phone started to ring in his pocket, but he ignored the call. 'You think that's why I was there at Andrew's office? I was looking for *you*. I came to *help*.'

She snorted with derision. 'Help yourself to my career, sure…'

Jacob's eyes widened. Grabbing the door handle to the store cupboard, he pulled her inside after him.

It was basically a huge white room, fitted out with shelves of racking containing various medical supplies. As soon as they were through the door he closed it behind them and backed away. Sitting on the floor, his back resting against one of the shelves, he took out his phone and checked the display before tapping out a message and putting it back in his pocket.

'I need this job too, Michelle, but I am not out to damage another doctor's career to get it. I came to look for you because I was worried.'

'I'm fine,' Michelle countered, taking a seat on the floor next to him, careful to leave a gap between their bodies. 'I don't need looking after; I'm fine on my own. Have been for a while.'

She didn't elaborate on the car crash that had been her last relationship, wincing at how much she had already admitted. But it was done, and now she was in self-preservation mode more than ever. Scott had once called her a robot, among other things. He'd told her he'd come home from work one day to find a stranger with his girlfriend's face, rattling around like a shell-shocked ghost.

'When I saw you outside his office I thought you were there to tell him what had happened,' she said now.

Jacob shook his head, brushing his hair back from his face. He looked across at her and she felt his eyes boring into her. 'I want the job—but what happened in that room…it's all forgotten. I'll never mention it again.'

Michelle felt a punch in her gut at his words. She didn't *want* to forget everything. She would remember some aspects of it for ever. She thought of Andrew, so concerned. Of Becks, standing there and screaming at her to move. That orange scrub cap lying on the floor, covered in blood.

Whenever she got close to anyone, pain was the only outcome. Today was a prime example.

Andrew probably blamed her for Becks. He knew, and he was holding it over her, trying to get her to talk. She wanted to tell him, but she couldn't. She couldn't tell anyone. She would rather curl up and die like her friend.

*I'm sorry, Becks. I talked you into coming with me. I needed you there and it cost you your life.*

'Start again? Clean slate?' said Jacob.

He was holding out his hand for her to shake, and she clasped it in hers. 'Deal. No more fighting.'

'Or head-butting,' Jacob added, and she couldn't help but laugh when she looked at his swollen face.

'No head-butting. I am *very* sorry,' she added, reaching out to stick down a tiny piece of dressing that had come undone.

He closed his eyes at her touch and she pulled away, moving to the door before he could open his lids again.

'Hey, not so fast, Zidane. I have one condition, for my silence.'

*A condition? Play it cool, Mich.*

'Zidane?' she queried, turning back to face him.

He grinned, his lips forming a perfect shape as he teased her. 'World Cup 2006. Zidane head-butted Materazzi. Keep up.'

She smiled despite herself. 'Nerd.'

'I prefer jock nerd, actually.' He pointed at his temple. 'I have brains *and* brawn.'

'Really?' She guffawed. 'Who told you that? Your mother? Mothers have to tell you that, you know, even if you turn out to be Billy Bragger.'

He looked affronted, giving an exaggerated snapping back of his head, a theatrical gasp. '*Someone's* deflecting!' he sang out in the space.

A faint echo sang back, taunting her in stereo.

'Go on—ask me what my condition is. I dare you.'

Michelle swallowed, the gulp ringing in her ears. She wouldn't back down though. Not. A. Chance. She made her body relax. Some days her stomach ached and her shoulders cramped with the effort of keeping herself looking 'normal' on the outside whilst wrestling her demons on the inside. Her whole body was suffering, coiled like a stress-filled spring.

'Go on then, Mr Perfect, what's your condition? Charity football match? Doing your charts for a week?'

He looked straight at her, his jaw tensing before he spoke. 'You won't like it.'

'Try me, Jacob. I'm a big girl.'

'You see a therapist here. Five sessions, then we're quits.'

Later that night she headed to the car park and threw her bags into the back seat. It was a very cool night for April, so she flicked on the heater to full blast. Turning on the ignition made her CD player spring into life once more, and she flicked it off. She'd been listening to her road trip mix that morning, but after the long day and night she couldn't bear to hear a single note.

The memories were just too heavy in the air tonight—like the ghosts of the departed, unseen and unfinished. The hospital stood before her, its hundreds of windows giving out light, containing loss and love and all the emotions in between. This place was her battlefield now, and she wanted to fight for it as much as she wanted to run away. She was broken, and St Marshall's was where people came to heal.

She could heal herself, stick herself back together within those walls. Every saved life was another Elastoplast applied to her own inner wounds. She would do it for Becks, for

Smithy—for all of them. Therapy, though? Did she really need that? Why did everyone seem to be getting at her? Was she worse than she thought at hiding her pain?

As she pulled out of the car park she didn't see the man standing in one of the windows at the hospital, looking out at her. She drove on unaware. Her head full of broken soldiers, violent dreams and stolen kisses.

# CHAPTER SIX

PICKING A CLUMP of sticky sugar off his elbow, Jacob came jogging down the plush carpeted staircase of his new house and sighed when he caught sight of the multitude of boxes piled up in the dining room.

He'd wanted to be ready for his early shift, and also fit in a jog on the way, but coming face to face with how much he had avoided unpacking was sobering to his good mood.

The truth was, not a lot of his bachelor lifestyle would transfer well to this new house. Framed art posters, trophies and awards from his marathons and surgical achievements…they were all so at odds with the person who had bought this place. He felt like a jumble of different people, all trying to get a hold on their new life.

He felt different. He'd woken up this morning happy, despite his lack of sleep. His nose was sore, and it had kept him awake last night, but the last few days had been interesting, to say the least. The more he learned about his co-worker—his rival for the top job—the more conflicted he was. And dare he say…aroused?

The thought of her all dressed up, out of her scrubs and without her usual guarded stance, stirred something deep within him. She had been a revelation that night of the party, and that night in the on-call room… He wanted to know more, to see more. He wanted to know what made her tick…why she was so adamant about getting the job.

Why did she want it? Was it just about winning? Ambition? Wouldn't she get bored eventually?

She struck him as the type of woman who would tire easily, work with the comfort zone of a role and then kick like hell against it. He was the same: living life to the full, hopping on planes at a moment's notice to save a life, helping the survivors of natural disasters.

They were cut from the same piece of adrenaline-soaked cloth, so her actions now were confusing to him. As confusing as his own must be to those who knew him in the profession. Was she that far gone?

She hadn't answered him yesterday, when he'd laid out his condition. His price for his silence. He'd braced himself for a kick-off, a battle with the fiery temptress who kept his thoughts jumbled and his head turned. She'd just left, though. Left him sitting there in the storeroom like an idiot.

The next time he'd seen her, it had been as though it had never happened. At one point Jacob had even wondered whether she had an evil twin. The two sides of her were so different that he couldn't reconcile them as being the same person.

Heading to the kitchen, he flicked on his coffee maker—one of the few things he had got around to unpacking from his old apartment. He'd mostly left his bachelor life boxed up. It was at odds with his new life with Ebony. The two worlds just didn't connect, but he was working on evolving. A lot faster than he'd expected to as well, thanks to Michelle. She had awoken something in him he hadn't known was there in the first place.

Nothing happened when he hit the button, and Jacob frowned. Then he saw the nanny had left a note stuck to the front of the machine.

*Out of filters. Have added to shopping list.*

He flicked the note, grateful that she was on the ball at least, but that wouldn't get him coffee.

'Dad?'

His little girl was standing in the doorway of the kitchen, looking cute in her soft cotton onesie. She slept like an explorer, loving to wrap herself in soft fabrics that held her skin tight and gave her the sensory feedback that made her feel centred.

'Morning, munchkin,' he said, glaring once more at the coffee machine and then looking back at her. 'It's a little early. You want some breakfast?'

As soon as he spoke, he felt his panic rise.

'Toast, please,' she said, walking up to the breakfast nook and trying to pull herself onto a stool. He watched her, unsure whether to help or not, but she soon got herself up. Giving her a weak smile, he opened the bread bin and was relieved to find half a small loaf in there. Thank goodness for the nanny.

Making Ebony some toast, he started to rummage around in his cupboards for some jam.

Everything was still alien to him here. Most nights by the time he got home he was too tired for much, and Ebony would already be asleep, adding to his guilt. At least before Steph had left she'd had a parent who knew where the jam lived, and her home hadn't been filled with boxes.

After the first few days of them being a family of two, Jacob had reeled. He was still reeling, frankly. He'd been summoned from the scene of a battle to face a different one back home. A mother who wanted her life and her freedom. A daughter who needed a home, a family. And the realisation that the disconnect between them was too wide to repair.

The first nanny he'd hired had quit. Probably due to the fact that she'd been dumped with the fractious autistic daughter of a surgeon who barely knew how much work being a full-time single parent was and seemed to dash off far too often.

Looking at Ebony now, eating toast and drinking juice while watching something on her tablet, he felt that twinge again. As soon as Susan arrived—the wonderful nanny who had dug her hands in deep and pulled their home into some sort of order—he'd have to go again. To fight for a job he needed, but didn't want to take from a woman he respected. A woman he craved a little. It was all very perplexing—and before coffee too.

He sat down next to his daughter and kissed the top of her head, avoiding her headphones.

'Daddy,' she said sweetly, 'it's bake sale day at school today. Did you get the things from the shop?'

*Jesus.* The text last night. He remembered now.

The kids were holding a bake sale after school, raising funds for more sensory equipment. So he'd called at the supermarket on the way home, throwing things from an online recipe into his trolley and heading home. Then Jacob had spent three hours in the kitchen, turning out crappy batch after crappy batch of cupcakes.

The first ones he'd burnt to a crisp; the second and third had turned out to have salt instead of sugar in them. The fourth batch were edible but looked like roadkill—leading to him downing a shot of tequila to recover.

'I did, honey, but Daddy's not a good baker.'

Turning to his little girl, he started to apologise, holding the plastic box of bashed buns in his hand. Ebony's little face was so innocent, he felt his heart squeeze once more.

*You're failing, Jacob. Get it together. Do better.*

He knelt down in front of her, putting the box to one side and pulling her onto his lap. 'I'm trying, sweetie. Maybe we should buy some cakes, or Daddy can donate some money?'

Ebony looked at him with her little blank face, leaning in and dropping a kiss on his cheek. 'It's okay, Daddy. Don't worry.'

The front door opened, startling them both, and Susan bustled in. Taking in the uncharacteristically calm morning scene before her, she recovered herself well and raised a carrier bag full of shopping.

'Baking day, Ebony, and we're all set! I made some buns for my Charlie, and I made too many! Do you want some for school?'

Ebony squealed, jumping off Jacob's lap and hugging Susan. Jacob tipped his buns into the trash before they noticed. *Phew.*

Susan pulled a bag of coffee filters out of the

bag and pushed it into Jacob's arms. He cradled it like a newborn baby.

'Thanks, superhero,' he said to her, and she patted him on the shoulder.

Ebony was back with her headphones on now, and she dodged half of his goodbye kisses but laughed when he pulled one of his silly faces.

'I'll be back late.' He said this to Susan, but he looked straight at his daughter when he spoke. 'Have a good day.'

He'd take a coffee with him, walk to work, see his new neighbourhood...maybe shake off the residual daddy guilt that seemed to have come with the territory the moment the stick had turned blue.

The old Jacob hadn't exactly been the type to put down roots, that was for sure. He'd bought and sold apartments every couple of years, moving on to the next job, the next project. Now he had gone and bought a house, with a garden and a drive—white picket fence territory.

He hadn't even told anyone at work about Ebony, and he was feeling more terrified about that than ever. He had planned to start telling people once he'd settled in, sure that he'd be able to pull it off for the meantime, till they found some kind of groove back home. When Michelle had come, that idea had gone out of the window. Now he was waiting for the right moment.

At this time in his life he needed that job, needed to be here—but what about Michelle? Would he even *want* the job after the battle that lay ahead? Now he had worked with her, it wasn't so easy to see what it would be like without her. The whole thing was giving Jacob a headache—but this time he wasn't running. Those days were gone, replaced with mortgages and bedtimes and baking supplies.

For now, he would settle for taking in the scenery.

One of the docs at the hospital had signed his broken nose off and he was fit for work, as long as he was careful, and he found himself picking up his usual leisurely pace through the park, backpack swinging from his shoulders.

He wanted to get to the hospital and punch in—and see the girl who had punched him out in more ways than one.

Definitely a knockout.

Forty minutes later, freshly dressed and in his

uniform of sharp suit and white coat, he headed for the nurses' station to see who was already clocked in. Looking at the trauma board, he saw that Michelle's name had been marked as offsite for the day and her OR schedule was empty. *What?* Was this because of the other night? Jacob felt a lurch in his stomach. Was that it? Had she been suspended?

'Is Dr Forbes off today?' He collared a passing nurse—Wendy something. 'There's nothing on the board?'

Wendy shrugged. 'I don't know what to tell you. Andrew has covered her shift today, cancelled all non-emergencies. She's out the whole day.' She stood a little straighter, pushing her chest out and giving him her best smile. 'Anything else you need?'

Distracted, Jacob muttered his thanks and turned on his heel towards Andrew's office.

'You're welcome,' Wendy said, and sighed, heading on her way.

Jacob, oblivious to her simpering, was just outside Andrew's office door, hand up ready to knock, when his boss opened the door and walked straight into him.

'Jacob,' he said smoothly. 'I was just coming to find you. Dr Forbes isn't in today, so I'm afraid it's up to you to step up.' He spotted Jacob's healing injury, a deep frown marring his features. He pointed towards Jacob's nose. 'Did you get that in A&E, by any chance?'

Jacob shook his head, but didn't elaborate. He felt a strong instinct to protect Michelle, to give her a chance to consider his request. He owed her that as a fellow combat medic.

*It's nothing to do with the kiss—or her. I'm giving her a chance. She gets help, we fight for the job, and that's it.*

He didn't want to push his brain into thinking any more deeply about the issue because he feared he might be lying to himself.

Was he at a disadvantage too? Mentally? He sure felt that way.

He didn't know what the hell he was doing as a man, but as a doctor he was clear. He wanted this job—he wanted to win it fair and square. What happened after that was anyone's guess, and his heart started to pound at the thought.

Exiting the lift on the third floor felt like entering a bubble. The moment the lift doors opened

Michelle was enveloped by the calm, almost numb energy that emanated from every facet of this department. The lights were warm and dim. There was no rushing around, no screams of pain, no blood on the floor from an arterial spray or a knife wound. Everything seemed to be slowed down—Michelle included.

She was already feeling odd, being dressed in her civilian clothes at her place of work, naked without her armour, but she had dressed in her favourite jeans and a cute top instead, slinging her running gear into a backpack, with a new pair of trainers she was going to break in.

By the time she had walked down the long corridor towards the man in a shirt and tie sitting behind the reception desk she felt as if she was having to really pull her feet off the floor with each step, as though she was wading through treacle to get there. Her jaw felt wobbly, breakable, and as the man turned to look at her with an easy open smile she stalled.

'Can I help?' he asked, giving her a broad, welcoming grin and his complete attention.

*Okay, so he's definitely in the right job. Now I just need to get the words out.*

'I have an appointment at eight a.m. Michelle Forbes.'

His face lit up in recognition and his smile widened.

*Maybe they gave the staff free samples of happy pills here.*

'Yes, Dr Forbes, I'll let Dr Colton know you're here. Do take a seat.'

She sat down on a comfortable-looking easy chair in the corner, away from any other people who might come in and wait. Her phone beeped in her pocket and she flashed the receptionist an apologetic look. He waved her away with another dentist-approved flash of teeth.

It was Wendy, messaging her to check if she was okay. She'd not told anyone where she was going. She tapped out a message saying that she was fine, and was in the building, but not on shift. She knew she'd been seen this morning, and that word would get around, but it wouldn't be from Wendy. She wasn't the type.

Michelle pressed 'send' and sat watching the dots flick across the bottom of the screen as Wendy replied.

Heads-up: Mr Trauma God has been looking for you.

She smiled to herself. Even when she was away, the others in her team had her back. She knew Jacob would never have an easy ride with them around, no matter the outcome of the job race. The hospital would be in good hands either way.

The happy receptionist's phone buzzed. 'You can go in now, Doctor.'

Michelle gulped, standing and nodding her thanks. She kept her head held high, her hands by her sides. Her fingers found a bruise-free piece of skin on her left leg, and before she walked towards the room she pinched herself. Hard.

*Still here. Alive. You feel that pain? That's good. That's nerve-endings telling you you're alive, safe, and in pain. Pinch. Now, walk, soldier. Left. Pinch. Right. Pinch.*

Taking a deep, shaky breath, she wrapped her free hand around the brushed steel door handle. It had taken her a long time to pluck up the courage to make the appointment, let alone get up this morning and drive here. Jacob's challenge had been the tipping point, though: she wouldn't welch on a bet, and that had given her the impetus she'd needed to finally pick up the phone. She hadn't told Jacob, and he'd never mentioned it.

They had worked together well since Lucas—watching over each other as they worked, pulling together when they needed to—and their working practice was tight and efficient now. They were equally tenacious about medicine, about saving lives, and Michelle had come to realise that there was no bigger turn-on than working with him when the chips were down. After a couple of stabbing victims had rolled in, leaving them both fighting to save people all day, it had taken everything she had not to jump him.

It was a welcome distraction from the perpetual gnaw of anxiety she carried deep in her gut. The way he made her feel involved different body parts altogether. It was frustrating, to say the least, but it had pulled her out of her fog just enough for her to lift her head towards fresh air. She needed to do this now—for her and for him. For her patients. For herself. For Becks.

She needed to stop blaming herself for Becks's death. She hadn't killed her, and she would have given anything to save her. She needed to put her friend to rest—but she didn't have the first clue how to do that. How to feel like herself again. Jacob had made her wake up, but his connection to Becks, their rivalry for the job… It was all a tangled ball of yarn in her head. She needed to find the end and start to unravel the mess. For everyone's sake.

'Everything okay?' the chirpy receptionist checked.

She had been staring at the door handle in her hand for the last few minutes, as though it would open the door to another world. Perhaps it would.

That thought got her moving.

'Not really,' she admitted finally, giving him a smile that she felt sure came across as a sad grimace. 'But I'm here. Gotta start somewhere.'

'No! Get off me!'

Little Benjamin Johnston wasn't having any of it. He didn't want to be tickled, he wouldn't let them lubricate his head, and he didn't even flicker so much as an eyelash in Jacob's direction now, as he produced a lollipop from the jar at the nurses' station.

'Don't want it!' he screamed, little fists clenched as he fully embraced his tantrum.

His mum was trying every trick she could—setting off the little siren on his favourite fire engine toy, pulling funny faces, threatening to call his nana…

*Right, I'm going in.*

'You don't want to be upsetting Nana, do you, Ben?' He kept his voice light, understated, but tinged with authority.

*We do not negotiate with toddlers.*

'If you let me have a look I'll only be a minute. Do you know how long a minute is? I bet you do, being such a big boy.'

Ben, clad in blue dungarees and a red-and-white-striped T-shirt, stopped his tight-fisted scream-fest just long enough to give Jacob a sideways glance. The potty-training toilet seat he was currently wearing as a hat didn't move as he turned his head. Jacob could see the tufts of hair sprouting up around the lodged plastic seat.

His mother whispered out of the corner of

her mouth. 'Keep talking—that's the first time he's been quiet in four hours.'

Jude, the nurse standing behind Mrs Johnston, waggled her finger in her ear. 'Thank Christ for that; I thought I'd gone deaf.'

Jacob slowly moved closer to him, walking on bended knee to reach his eye level. The little lad was cute when he wasn't holding the trauma department hostage. A&E had sent him over, due to overcrowding and complaints from the other patients in the emergency waiting room.

'I tell you what, young Ben…'

Ben jerked a little at the sound of Jacob's voice, and his little fists clenched tighter, his mouth opening to show five little pearly-white teeth poking through his gums. He started to draw a breath…

'Oh, Lord, not again,' his mother wailed.

'Jesus, I am *never* having kids,' Jude muttered, patting Mrs Johnston on the back soothingly.

Ben straightened his back, taking a deep breath and using every bit of his two-foot-something stature to impress upon them his frustration. 'No!' he shouted. 'Potteeee!'

Then it clicked. Jacob had a vision pop up

in his head: Ebony, sitting on a plush cream-and-yellow-striped runner, screaming because her favourite character-emblazoned shoes were dirty. He never knew what to do. He got it now—even if he hadn't then. His daughter's tantrums and meltdowns over the years had opened his eyes. Sometimes, you just had to think outside the box.

He looked over his shoulder at the nurses, talking to them out of the corner of his mouth. They all strained to hear him, leaning forward as he instructed them what to do.

Jude's eyes lit up. 'I have just the thing—wait there.'

She dashed out of the room whilst Ben screeched on, his big sad eyes looking at them the whole time, not letting anyone near him.

Jacob looked across at Mrs Johnston and sighed. She was sitting there, hugging her bag, talking softly to Ben, trying to console him, trying to distract him, to make him laugh. He was having none of it. And when she tried for a hug it only made him louder and more agitated. She looked exhausted, and embarrassed, and a little beaten down.

Not for the first time Jacob found himself

wondering why people did it. The whole parenting thing. To him, it seemed like a lifetime of worry, of always being 'on call', of always having that gnawing fear.

Looking at Mrs Johnston now, he couldn't help but feel sorry for her. Maybe he was throwing a little pity party for himself too—not that he could ever speak out loud how he felt. It just wasn't done…

'Got it! You're lucky it's curry night Chez Jude.' Jude trotted back in, brandishing a big white pot of coconut oil.

Ben's mother's face was a picture. 'Will that work?' she asked, looking from medical professional to medical professional.

Jacob gave her an easy smile. 'Distraction is a powerful weapon,' he said, and it hit him how true that was in his own life.

He'd felt constantly distracted since he met the ball of chaos that was Michelle. He even found himself thinking of her now, but he pushed her out of his mind. Ben's screams and general hatred for everyone around him helped to quiet the noise of the woman in his head.

'Ladies, get ready. I'm going in…'

Taking the pot from Jude, Jacob sat down on

the floor near to Ben and slowly unscrewed the cap. The other nurses left to attend to their patients, leaving the four of them alone. Slowly Jacob rubbed some of the coconut oil from the pot into his own hair, making it stick up at odd angles.

Ben side-eyed him, and the cacophony of shouts and moans slowly subsided, as though someone had found his remote control. Mrs Johnston sighed audibly with relief, and Jacob winked at her.

He dipped his finger into the pot again, pulling out more this time and rubbing it between his fingers before slapping it all over his hair. When he caught his reflection in the mirror on the wall he saw he looked like a mad professor—and he saw something else too: Michelle. She was standing—well, peeking—in the doorway, in civilian clothes, watching him.

He felt his heart thud in his chest and looked away quickly. Knowing she was watching him work felt like showcasing his skills, showing her that she could trust him, and that meant a lot to him.

He didn't want to probe the reasons why it mattered so much. Why his interaction with this child was something he wanted her to see. That was another thought for another sleepless night, with the sheets wrapped around his sweat-slicked body.

He'd used to sleep better out there, on tour, which was crazy, really. But many a night he had slept like a newborn babe, lulled into slumber by the sounds of unrest all around him. He'd felt part of something there; here, he'd just felt…lost. Powerless, even. Overwhelmed. Until her.

Ben padded over, his feet now bare after an earlier shoe and sock purge, and Jacob held the pot out to him. Ben looked at him, then back at the pot, and then his little fingers were in the sweet-smelling waxy mixture. Pulling out a covered hand, he laughed, holding it up for them both to see.

'Yeah, that's it, little man—like this!'

Jacob rubbed oil into his hair again, following the rough shape of the potty seat that was stuck to Ben's head. After a moment Ben started to rub it into his own hair, and Jacob took that as a signal.

Getting another good handful ready, he shuffled forward, hands raised to warn Ben what was coming. 'Now, let's get that off, dude, and go get you a lollipop.'

Ben took the signal and, leaning forward, rubbed his little hands on Jacob's head. His hair was now almost crunchy with the mixture, but it was worth it. In return Jacob massaged oil into the little boy's head, gently pulling and testing the seat's level of tightness as he went. A few more rubs and the seat started to give. Ben shoed no sign of being distressed; in fact, he was beckoning his mother to come and play.

'One more little…' Jacob pulled again, and this time the seat came free.

Ben barely noticed; he was having too much sticky-fingered fun.

His mum burst into tears on the spot. 'Oh, my God, I can't believe you got it off! Thank you!'

She hugged Ben, laughing as he grabbed her face in coconut-scented hands, giving her a big kiss. His earlier bad mood was forgotten, and all was right in his little world.

'It's no bother,' Jacob said, smiling at them both broadly.

The feeling of having helped someone, changing someone's day for the better, was always a high, and he basked in it now.

He waggled the potty seat at them. 'I'd recommend not using these again. I hate the things. Never worked for me.' *This was it. This was his chance.* 'My daughter hated them too—and potties.'

Ben's mum rolled her eyes conspiratorially at him. 'I can relate. What worked in the end?'

Jacob opened his mouth to answer but realised that he didn't know. The truth was, he'd gone away on tour, leaving a stubborn Ebony with her frustrated mother, Jenny—a nurse he'd been seeing on and off for a while…nothing serious.

Until she'd fallen pregnant and he had stepped up. Or tried to.

He and Jenny had had nothing in common other than a basic physical attraction and jobs with unsociable hours. Bringing a child up together, living together…it had been complicated. In the end Jenny had left—and he had come home and stepped up.

'Perseverance, I guess,' he said, as truthfully as he could. 'You're there, doing it, helping him learn. That's all he needs. He'll get there with your help.'

She nodded, the anxiety and stress visibly falling away from her as she held her son close.

'You're doing a great job, Mrs Johnston. Don't worry—he's thriving.'

He remembered Michelle then, his heart thumping faster at the thought. He looked to the doorway but she was gone.

Another missed opportunity to add to the others.

Thank God for en-suite bathrooms in on-call rooms. Far better than a tarp, a few poles, and a bucket of water. Although even with cutting-edge bathroom facilities, it took Jacob a good twenty minutes of scrubbing and shampooing to get rid of the oil in his hair. He could still smell coconut in the air when he came out of the shower, throwing a towel around himself and grabbing another to dry his hair.

Heading out of the bathroom to the connected on-call room, he threw the second towel onto his head, drying his fragrant locks.

'You smell like the air after a tropical storm.'

The words came from nowhere, and Jacob jumped a foot and a half in the air, his head still encased in the towel, his limbs flailing against the intruder.

He spun around, wrestling wildly with the towel around his head. He managed to pull it off at the very same second as the bath sheet around his torso fell down, hitting the deck and leaving him standing there butt naked.

He looked for the voice and there she was. Michelle. Lying on her side on the far bed, propped up on one elbow, looking at him open-mouthed, her expression showing as much shock as he felt.

'I…er…' he began.

'Oh, I'm so…'

They both stopped, the ends of their sentences floating in the air around them like wisps of snaking smoke.

'I didn't think anyone was going to be in here…sorry,' he said, once he had the power of speech.

She nodded, a little smile playing on her features. 'That's okay, I sneaked in. I don't really feel like going home, to be honest.'

She looked him up and down, her eyes drinking him in. He let her—and then he realised he hadn't picked up the towel.

'Oh, God—still naked!' He cursed, scrabbling for the towel and wrapping himself up again.

'Aw…' Michelle said, surprising him. 'Show's over, eh?' She pulled a silly face, laughing again when he blushed furiously. She stood up, heading towards the door. 'I'll let you get changed.'

She reached for the door at the same time he did, and just as quickly as it had opened, it clicked shut.

'Don't go,' he found himself saying. 'Stay— just for a little while. I have something to tell you, actually. I tried to tell you earlier…in a way.'

He walked his fingers along the polished wood surface of the door, brushing his hand against hers and threading his fingers through hers. They stood just inches apart, each with one hand on the door, turned towards each other.

He wanted to tell her about his daughter, about how wrongly she had read him, but he couldn't articulate anything that was flashing through his brain into actual words. He felt as if his skin was on fire, and his chest was rising and falling rapidly from the shock of his sheer need for her. Looking at her, he knew she felt it too. Her pupils were dilated in the charged darkness of the room.

'I should let you get on,' she tried feebly, but she made no move to leave. 'Tell me later.'

'I have time,' he said, his voice thick with lust. Then he thought of her being MIA earlier, and felt his heart clench. 'Where were you today?'

A shadow crossed her features. 'Third floor. Head shrinkers.'

He saw then how pale she was, how drawn. She'd done it; she'd taken the first step. He felt a surge of pride swell in his chest, and a rush of something else not far behind.

'Why? Did you miss me?' she added, her lips pushing out into a little faux pout.

*She's teasing me*, he realised with a jolt. *Careful, Jacob, this is not the time to start anything. You need to tell her. Think of the job...think of...*

She closed the gap between them before he had a chance to react. Her lips closed on his in a soft, gentle kiss that was over before it began. *Blink and you'd miss it.* Jacob would have happily surgically removed his eyelids so as not to miss that moment again.

She pulled away, and it took every ounce of his self-control for him not to lunge for her, to take her into his arms, show her what was under that towel again.

'Well, I think *you* missed *me*,' he quipped, before his playful look could turn to want again. 'You okay?'

He looked into her eyes and could see that she was miles away again. Probably back in that room, having to lay out the bones of her past for a clinical stranger. It was a lot, but he knew she could take it. Getting a handle on it was the first priority.

He saw her free hand fall to her side, pinching the skin on her leg through her clothing. He turned to face her square-on, their toes kissing each other through her shoes. Taking the hand away from her thigh, he took it in his and, bringing it up to his face, kissed it.

'You're not alone, you know,' he told her.

Once upon a time that would have been his stock response—telling people that he was there, that there was a light at the other side, to hang on. No man left behind. Or woman. Especially not one he was rapidly falling for, head over heels.

She made him want to be better, to try harder, to push himself to go that extra mile. She challenged him, excited his senses, made him hard at the mere flash of her skin or the touch of her lips. He was standing in front of her and he couldn't think of any better place to be. He wanted to help her. He needed her to recover from this, to be whole again. He needed it because *she* did. Anything less than one hundred percent was just not good enough for people like them. They were cut from the same cloth.

'I'm here.'

'That's half the problem,' she muttered, a flash of humour rolling across her features.

'Now, now...' Jacob chided, pulling her closer. 'I think having me around isn't so bad after all. You just won't admit it because you're as stubborn as they come.' He saw her mouth drop, and he laughed softly. 'Gotcha!'

She smirked in response, making him want to kiss her again, to make her legs wobble. He liked the challenge she represented, but in a very different way from the way he'd liked his previous conquests. They had been a diversion, a way of scratching an itch, a moment of shared comfort in a tormented war zone, a distraction from playing unhappy family at home, where he'd co-parented a child as one of two people who had just been making the best of a one-night stand with consequences.

Michelle was more than that.

Jenny was off doing her own thing now, her daughter and her ex-lover firmly in her rear view mirror. Jenny was nothing like Michelle. Michelle was something to strive for—not a short-term crutch to see him through the night.

She opened her mouth to speak, and surprised him all over again. 'What did you mean earlier, when you were talking about the potty seat?'

*She knows I saw her.*

'You sounded like you had some experience in the matter.'

'You saw that?' he asked, feigning ignorance for just a minute longer. 'How much did you hear?'

She shrugged. 'Just that you hated those potty seats. I got called away. Cute kid, wasn't he? Hard work, though. I can't imagine having to cope with tantrums like that day in, day out. Makes our job look a little easier, doesn't it?' She laughed a little. 'My niece is gorgeous—

don't get me wrong—but that kid was another level today.'

She giggled again, and Jacob's plan to tell her about Ebony clanged shut in his mind like a steel cell door.

'I've seen it happen before,' he said, his voice weak and flat. 'The best time was when a dad got one stuck on his head, trying to dance for his kid to get him to use the potty.'

And also another time. A screaming little girl going red in the face because she hadn't been able to cope with what was being asked of her.

He would hear those sobs till the last day he drew breath. That was the moment they'd known Ebony was different. Not worse—just different. They'd been told Ebony was autistic, and his impending tour had made things so much worse for all three of them.

'Do you want kids someday?' he asked, holding his breath for her answer.

'Sure,' she said, nodding at him. 'Someday when things settle down, maybe. I always thought I would—but this life, you know…?'

He nodded, trying to hide his swirling emotions of relief and worry. 'Yeah, I know. I actually—'

A laugh sounded at the other side of the door, followed by a crash and a cheer. The universal sound of someone with butterfingers. Michelle had turned her face towards the door, her work brain clicking on and assessing the noise. He watched her, saw the frown lines on her forehead deepening as she strained to listen for any danger.

'It's probably Wendy—that woman would never make a juggler,' he muttered, leaning closer till their foreheads touched.

He needed to touch her, to comfort her, and he couldn't stop himself any longer. She let him, and even pulled him closer, a soft laugh escaping her.

He snapped, unable to take any more. 'What are we *doing*, Mich?'

He felt like a teenager—all hormones and insecurities. How did she do it? She had him, an alpha male, wrapped around her surgical-gloved finger, and the best thing was she had no idea. For the first time in Jacob's rather daring life he felt vulnerable, exposed, and he didn't even care. Not when it came to her.

She was biting her lip now, her eyes on the floor, and he used his left index finger to raise her chin, to make her eyes meet his. He wanted her to *be* his, to know about Ebony, to understand what kind of man he was, what kind of father he was trying to be. He needed her to see him through the blood and the loss and the fear. The way he had seen her.

*PTSD loves company—go figure.*

'Michelle, what is this? What are we doing?' he asked again. He could feel his heart pounding in his chest, sounding the drums of love loud in the silent room. 'Do you feel this? Do you feel for me what I feel for you?'

It was out there. The question he had wanted to ask since that first night. She had broken his nose, and now he was terrified she would break his heart too. He held his breath.

'Yes,' she said, looking him straight in the eye.

She had never looked so sexy.

'I feel it too.'

He didn't wait a second longer. Reaching behind him, not moving his gaze from hers, he clicked the lock on the door. Slowly he ran his fingers up the sides of her cheeks, taking her face in his hands and touching his lips to hers. She tasted sweet, and he kissed her again, moving his mouth from her lips to the side of her neck, running his tongue along her clavicle, pulling her top out of the way and growling in his throat when he was rewarded with a peek of black lacy bra and pink skin.

He reached the end of her shoulder and nipped her, just once, with his teeth. The resulting moan from her spurred him on, and he put his broad arms around her, lifting her off the ground. She wrapped her legs around him readily, her back now pushed against the on-call room door, his body slotted against hers, till only the clothing they wore separated them.

She moved her arms around his shoulders, running her fingers through his hair, giving it a sharp tug and pulling his mouth against hers once more.

The kiss ignited as they both fully gave in to sensation. Mouth on mouth, tongue caressing tongue… They moaned and panted as they kissed each other passionately, exploring each other with everything they had. He tried to wrap his hands tighter around her and growled in frustration.

'The bed,' she muttered into his mouth, barely breaking the kiss.

He whirled her around, walking her in his arms, still locking lips with her, and laid her down on the bed, lying down alongside her. She moved position, pushing him till his back hit the mattress. He let her take the lead, not quite believing how things had gone from him being covered in coconut oil and keeping secrets to being here, kissing her in the on-call room, touching this woman who wanted the job he needed.

She looked at him, her lips swollen from their kiss, and put her hand on his chest, over the space where his heart lived. He covered it with his own hand, linking their fingers together and pulling her closer. She came easily, her legs astride him now, so she was sitting on him, her hair ruffled, sexy. She looked him straight in the eye and started to pull her top up.

Jacob leaned forward, resting on his elbows, kissing the skin that she uncovered. Her stomach—flat and still tanned—her ribs—one side and then the other. He left a trail of hot kisses all the way up her body, reaching up and cupping her through her black bra. She let him, moving her body closer to his touch, rubbing herself against him, those pieces of fabric the only barrier.

She moved to take the towel away, and he rose with her, helping her, giving her access to every inch of him. The towel dropped off the bed and Michelle drank him in. He lay there beneath her, letting her feast on him, enjoying the sensations evoked by having her this close. There wasn't a drug rep in the world who could sell him anything that would top this. It was pure, wild… And, whatever they were doing, if they went any further there would be no going back.

He moved slowly, bringing her with him till they were sitting up, her legs wrapped around him, his arms around her. Only her bra and her jeans to go now, but he wasn't going to make the first move. It had to be her, on *her* terms. For once Jacob found himself enjoying relinquishing control to someone else.

'This is a bad idea…' she said, running her fingers along Jacob's bare chest, leaning forward to lick the glistening drops of water still left from the shower.

He flinched at her touch and his muscles tensed. She laughed, running her tongue along his side now, along the bumps of his abs, clearly enjoying the feeling of him bucking and writhing beneath her.

'Insanely bad...' he breathed, pulling her mouth back to his and kissing her. He could feel himself hard beneath her, and he couldn't take much more. 'Do that again.'

She laughed, pushing him gently, with a poke of her finger in his chest, and he flopped back, undoing her bra with a well-practised flick of his wrist. From his position he could see the swell of her breasts under the fabric and he slowly pulled it off, her bright eyes following his movements. The piece of lace followed his towel to the floor and there she was, laid out before him.

It was then that he saw it—a scar, running down one side of her left breast, puckering the skin slightly as she moved to cover herself.

'No,' he said, shaking his head and gently taking her hands away, resting them on his chest again. 'Let me look at you.'

He ran a finger along the scar, seeing where the surgeon had tried to repair the injury as best he could. He knew from his training that this was a patch-up job, done with speed and skill, minimum tools and medicine. It was a battle scar and she clearly hated it. He could see it in her eyes, which were now looking at anything and everything in the room apart from him.

'You are absolutely perfect,' he murmured.

He'd only said that to one girl before today—Ebony—and both times he'd meant it as earnestly as any man ever had.

'Don't ever feel the need to hide any part of yourself. Especially not from me.'

He moved his head to one side, exposing the small silvery scar that ran along his collarbone. She gasped a little, running her thumb along it and making him want to kill whoever was stupid enough to have invented denim. He needed her so much it was painful.

'Shrapnel?' she checked, and he nodded.

'Qatar. Those last few days were pretty bad in our camp.'

He ignored the flash of his memory, the thought of his pain as the home-made bomb had exploded, showering them all with shards of jagged metal, nuts, bolts, pieces of old buildings. Anything that would cause the most damage. It could have been a lot worse. Jacob was grateful that the bomb-maker had been an inexperienced small child. Imagine being grateful for such a thing in this world.

'Yours?' he asked.

She was still self-conscious—he could tell. She lifted her left arm, bent it at the elbow so her fist rested on the ball of her shoulder. Red lines like jagged cuts ran along her side, where the skin was raised, still healing.

'Ambush. One of the people we were treating was being hunted, and the hunters came to camp to try to get him back.'

A single tear escaped her eye and ran down her cheek before she had a chance to stop it. It dripped from her cheek onto his muscular chest and she rubbed it away.

'I raised my arms to protect myself...took a chunk. I thought I'd lost my arm for sure.'

Another tear dripped down and he rubbed it with his thumb, lifting himself up to meet her chest to chest and kissing her tears away. She kissed him back, wrapping her arms around him again. Slowly he moved them both till he was on top of her, pinning her gently to the bed with his naked body.

'You're okay,' he murmured between kisses. 'You're here. You made it.'

'So did you,' she deadpanned back. 'Does that mean we really are out, though? Does anyone really get out?'

*What wasn't she telling him? What was hidden behind those cautious eyes?*

He didn't answer her with words, because he didn't want her to hear him lie. He answered her with his hands, moving them over her, bringing her closer to him. He wanted to unzip himself from head to toe, to take her into him and keep her close, the two of them together against the world with all its struggle and enemies.

They moved together, healing each other with their touch, and he whispered things into her ear, letting her open up to him in her own time. He knew she needed to be in control, and he was a willing passenger on her journey to recovery, to becoming fully herself once more.

He had so much to tell her, but this wasn't the time. He would speak to her with his body for now…show her what he couldn't utter with his voice.

'Do you have anything?' she whispered in his ear, nibbling at his neck as she went.

'In my trouser pocket,' he replied, suddenly

grateful that old habits died hard. 'A good soldier is always prepared.'

She raised a brow at him, and he wanted to take her there and then.

'On a promise?' she teased.

He laughed—a low rumble in his chest that made her body move with the movement. Her eyes rolled back a little and he grabbed her hips, moving her just once over his pelvis.

'A man needs to be ready for anything, but it's been a while.'

Arching a brow, she looked at him. 'How long?'

'Long enough. No more talking, Dr Forbes.'

She moaned, reaching across to the discarded clothes on the other bed and getting what she needed. Tearing open the packet, she took her time, with Jacob moaning about slow torture.

'You ready?' she asked, once he was sheathed and waiting.

'I was born ready, woman. Come here,' he growled, and reached for her.

## CHAPTER SEVEN

A BUZZING NOISE woke Michelle from her slumber. For once her sleep hadn't been full of terrors, and she hadn't even dreamed. She lifted her head a little, listening to the noise. On the other bed Jacob's pager was lit up, just visible clipped to his white coat. It wasn't the emergency tone, but it made her very aware of her surroundings all the same.

A stirring came from the side of her, and she turned to see Jacob lying on his back, naked, one arm underneath her back, pulling her close, the other holding her hand tight. She made a move to leave him, but in sleep he tightened his grip, mumbling to himself and making it harder for her to pull away.

She'd slept with a colleague. In the same on-call room where she had head-butted him and broken his nose just a short time ago. They were nearing the halfway mark in their race for the job, and now things were more complicated than ever.

*What the hell are you doing?*

Rebecca was somewhere laughing at her, no doubt. It gave her a pang to think of her friend. Had he whispered the same things to her? Used the same moves? But it didn't feel as if it was just lust, and he'd said all the right things. Could a man be a player one day and a relationship man the next?

She gently peeled herself away from him, dressing quickly and quietly. She needed to get up, get out of there, go home.

What if Andrew found out? Would they both lose their jobs before they'd even had a chance to prove themselves to the investors?

He moved, and she turned in panic. He was still asleep, smiling at something. She grabbed her things and then knelt by the bed, watching his long dark lashes flutter against his skin.

*What's in that handsome head of yours, Jacob? Can I really trust you? Do you really know how messed up I am? Do you know how messed up you are?*

She stroked the thick dark hair back from his forehead, exposing a tiny scar in his hairline that she hadn't seen before. She bent down, running her lips along it like a whisper in the dark.

She knew it shouldn't work. He was her rival, a player who had slept with a friend she still mourned, but she just couldn't leave him alone. She was starting to think about him all the time, wondering how he was, how his day was going, what his home looked like.

A knock came at the door, and she flinched. 'Dr Peterson?'

*Shit. The page must be urgent after all.*

She checked, but Jacob was still asleep. The pager went off again, but it was unnoticed by him. The man was exhausted.

She smiled a little, feeling a dirty kind of satisfaction that she might be the cause.

*We have a lot to talk about*, she thought to herself. *But maybe we just need to go for it.*

She stood, checking her hair quickly in the mirror. She looked as if she had just been thoroughly seen to—which wouldn't do at all. She smoothed it down as best she could, opening the door a crack. One of the receptionists was standing there—a temp whose name Michelle could never remember.

'Yes?' she said, in her firm doctor voice.

'Oh, sorry, Doctor.' The woman blushed, trying and failing to peek behind Michelle into the room. 'I thought Dr Peterson was in here.'

'He left a while ago,' she lied. 'Canteen. Is there an emergency case?'

The woman, a nervous, mousy-haired twenty-something, shook her head vigorously. 'No, nothing like that. I just need him to call home—can you tell him if you see him?'

Call home? It was then that Michelle noticed the little pink message the receptionist was holding in her hand. She eyed the scrawl but couldn't make it out. A cleaner, maybe? A contractor? People who lived alone like she did didn't get calls from home.

'No problem,' she said brightly, grabbing the piece of paper from her in a flash. She had to see it. The woman balked, but said nothing. 'I'll pass the message on. Thank you.'

She waved the woman away, closing the door slowly. One look at Jacob and she knew he was still fast asleep, his breathing slow and deep. She read the message, then crumpled it into a ball, tight between her shaking fingers.

*I can't believe I was so stupid.*

She looked around the room. Sheets and clothes tossed everywhere. Pillows on the floor. The smell of sex in the air. It felt so cheap now—a sordid and tawdry bunk-up at work, not a passionate meeting of bodies and minds.

She felt a wave of shame—and then came the anger. She'd done it now. The epic cock-up that would end everything she'd been clinging to. She had to leave immediately. She was just another trophy on his wall and she hated herself for falling for it.

She knew better; she always had. When she got close to someone it was for a reason, and it didn't come easily.

What was she going to do now? Why, just when she'd been able to see a glimpse of a future, had it been taken away? She couldn't handle it. She was going to break down right here and right now, and she was terrified that once she went down that road it was be hard to come back.

A solitary sob erupted from her, and she slapped herself hard across the face.

'Stop it!' she whispered to herself angrily. 'Stop it. Now. Pull. Yourself. Together.'

She punctuated each word with a sharp slap,

her other hand pinching her thigh over and over again, till she could barely stand the pain. *Better*, she thought as her nerve-endings screamed at her to stop.

Listening with one ear to the door for a moment, she checked the coast was clear. She slammed the door hard behind her and didn't stop until she was safely in her car, heading out of the car park with a screech of tyres.

She kept on pinching herself till she was safely locked behind her front door, and it was there, on the polished wood floor, that she finally fell apart and let the hot, salty tears flow freely.

*I'm alone*, she realised with a jolt, knowing that the reassuring solid presence of Jacob had been taken away in one pretty pink note. *I'm alone and I deserve to be. It's over. It's just all so…hopeless.*

'What?' Jacob blurted, flying out of bed and going from being fast asleep to standing there alert, arms out in a fighting stance, all in a few seconds. *'What?'* he barked again—before his vision and his brain caught up, processing the images.

A loud bang had woken him and now he was standing there in the buff, looking as if he was about to fight the door.

'Michelle?' he asked, but he knew she had left the room.

Her stuff was all gone...no note left. He rummaged in his clothing, throwing on his boxers and checking his pager. *Phew.* Nothing work-related. He frowned as he saw the group of messages so close together, frantic. He needed to call home.

He had been enjoying a dream—him at home with Ebony, and Michelle right there with them. But he felt bone-tired all of a sudden, and with a groan he headed back to the reality of the day.

The next day Michelle strode into a room on the third floor, slapping down the pink piece of paper in front of her very surprised therapist.

'Dr Forbes. I actually have a patient in—'

'Open up, you said. Trust someone, you said. Well, what do you say about *this*?'

She grabbed the note back from the coffee table, thrusting it into his face.

'Dr Colton, you suck at your job.'

She rolled the paper into a ball, throwing it

into the wastepaper basket at the side of her with a huff of disgust before flouncing down onto the leather couch opposite him.

'Firstly, I only have a few minutes before my next patient, and secondly, the name's Greg. What seems to be upsetting you?'

She pounded the sofa cushions with her fists, trying to get a grip on her anger. Mostly at herself. She had taken her eye off the ball and look what had happened. She'd become a notch on Dr Love's bedpost—a bedpost already so notched that it looked more like a set of tooth-picks than a trophy wall.

'I tried what you said. I tried reaching out.'

An image of Jacob's corded forearm, reaching down between their bodies, his hand pressing his thumb against her nub, sprang into her head.

*Get out, Lust MD. Today is angry woman day. I hope you got the memo.*

Greg Colton's face developed a slow, cautious smile. 'I see,' he said. 'And…?'

'Read the note, Doctor. I put myself out there and made a fool of myself. I failed—*again.*'

Greg said nothing as he unfolded the crumpled piece of paper, read it. His face remained the same, not changing expression.

*Damn, what is it with shrinks and their poker faces?*

He smoothed the paper out, tucking it into her client file and then sitting back down in his easy chair.

The note read.

*Chinese tonight? Hurry home.*
*Love you.*
*Call me.*
*Ebony*

'This is addressed to Dr Peterson. Is he the doctor who has your job?'

She nodded, wanting to disagree with him about the finer points of who had the job, but deciding against it. It *was* her job—although now the lines were even less clear.

'This is upsetting to you?'

*State the obvious, Greg.*

She rolled her eyes at him and he smiled, just a fraction, before those shutters came down again, disguising his thoughts.

'Yes,' she replied eventually. 'It does. He did this to Rebecca, you know.'

'Did what?' he asked.

'Slept with her…used her.'

Greg smiled kindly. 'From what you've told me about the situation, and your friend, it sounds to me like it was a mutual arrangement. Friends with benefits, as they call it. Do you *really* think he exploited her?'

She opened her mouth to say yes, but she knew it wasn't true. Rebecca had been a modern single woman; she'd known what she was doing the same as him.

'Still, he wasn't free like she was. He wasn't single and modern. He was just the same as half the men in the world. He went with his trouser brain. I should have known better.'

Greg's eyes narrowed, and he wrote something on a pad next to him just as the buzzer from Reception sounded.

'Dr Forbes, my patient is here, but I want to talk about this further. Are you available for a session tomorrow? It can start early if you need to work around a shift. Book in with Reception, okay?' He patted the note. 'We will start here tomorrow.' He sat back in his seat, making a steeple with his long fingers. 'The key point here is forgiveness, remember? You need to stop apologising for surviving, Michelle. It's hurting you.'

Michelle left, reluctantly making an appointment, and then heading to the lift to go down to the trauma floor. One floor lower and Andrew was standing there, waiting to get on.

'Hi,' he said jovially, waving his briefcase at her as they stood side by side, waiting for the lift doors to close. 'You okay?'

'Fine,' she said, giving him her best at-the-top-of-my-game smile. 'Ready to get going.'

Andrew beamed. 'Great! Jacob's clearly had the same idea. He's been like a man on a mission all morning.'

Michelle turned to look at him. She was an hour early for work, but Jacob was already here?

'What do you mean, on a mission...?'

Jacob Peterson was already walking on cloud nine when he spotted the lift doors opening and saw Andrew and Michelle standing there, deep in conversation. So deep that they didn't even realise the doors had opened.

What was the deal? Were they talking about

him? About the job? Was she filling him in on their recent interactions?

The more they stood there talking, the more Jacob felt his hackles rising. His paranoia was so large it felt like a full-sized companion, a shadow on his back. He'd never been scared of losing things before, and he wasn't doing well at it. When Ebony had needed him—when Jenny had said she was done with him, with her, with them—he had fought for her. He'd stepped up—albeit far too late. If he lost Michelle now he knew he wouldn't take it well.

He looked down at his sides and saw his fists were clenched tight.

*What was going on?*

Michelle was smiling at Andrew now, and Jacob wanted to slap him for being the lucky receiver.

As though his thoughts had summoned her, Michelle turned in that moment, stepping out of the lift and looking straight at him. She looked him up and down, her face neutral, and then, turning on her heel, she was gone, leaving Jacob still wondering what the hell was going on.

*She left you asleep in that room, naked. No note.*

An uncomfortable notion entered his head. Maybe she regretted it altogether. He hadn't considered that. He hadn't been left in bed before. He was the one who did the leaving—or he had been. Was that the look in her eye? Regret?

After all, they barely knew each other and they were fighting for the same job. Could it end well for either of them? Just because Jacob was ploughing on ahead, despite these nagging issues, it didn't mean that Michelle was able to. She had her own demons and problems to face—just as he did.

The difference was that her pain was on show and she was letting him in…just a little. He knew he couldn't say the same about himself. Would she be okay with his baggage if she knew about it? What would that look like?

There were too many questions to be answered. And in their line of work that was a dangerous thing. In trauma, you were fighting fires constantly. Patching people up, making things work, improvising—anything to shovel the sands of time back into the timer, giving their patients more time, another day to live and to be loved.

Jacob thrived on it, and he knew Michelle did too, but, in real life was a relationship built on adrenaline and rivalry doomed from the start?

The feel of her moving with him yesterday had told him differently. They'd fitted each other perfectly, knitting their kind of damage together and healing it, turning it into something different. Was a foundation of that kind enough to sustain a relationship?

Jacob knew he wanted to try. They had almost three weeks left and he was going to give it his all, let the chips fall where they may.

He didn't answer the loudest question of all. At the end of that time would he want the job, or his rival?

As he walked away to see his next patient he realised that it was all a moot point anyway. The fact was that she'd left, and now she was talking in corners with Andrew. And that look she'd just given him didn't bode well. It might well be that the woman who ran through his mind fifty times an hour would break his heart as well as take the job he needed.

It ruined his good mood for the day.

\* \* \*

Michelle looked at the OR board and cursed the light day. Then she cursed herself, for wishing for a bus crash or a small natural disaster to give her something to distract herself. She needed to have the feel of a scalpel in her hand as she worked to save a patient. She needed to get busy and bury her head in the sand.

Hell, the way she was feeling, she almost wished for the anonymity of the desert. Almost.

'Quiet day,' Jacob said, his deep voice making her body react.

*Traitor libido! Lock it up, Medic.*

He brushed his sleeves back from his wrists and loosened his tie. 'I've been wishing for a trauma. Is that bad?'

She laughed despite herself. 'It's pretty bad, yeah.'

He crossed his arms, showing off muscular forearms sprinkled with thick dark hair. She found herself wondering what his chest would look like if it was covered in hair...something to run her fingers through on a cold winter's night.

*Geez, woman, get a grip. You are too bad-*

*ass to be a puddle at some man's feet. Especially his.*

'I knew it. Where did you go yesterday?'

He lowered his voice, leaning in. She caught a whiff of his aftershave and felt her stomach flip.

'I had to get home; my place is a bit of a work in progress.'

She could have bitten her tongue off, but what else could she say? She couldn't exactly show him the telephone message, could she? Not only had she stolen it and not told him, she'd also tried to shame her therapist with it, and now it was hanging in her file like a big scarlet letter.

He pulled a business card out of his wallet, passing it to her as they both pretended to study the board. 'I didn't have your number, so here's mine.'

She looked at it in her hand, but didn't put it in her pocket right away. 'I have your pager number,' she said, and looked at him to judge his reaction.

He just looked confused. 'I know, but that's work stuff. I'd like to have your home number…to call you and take you out, maybe? We could actually talk outside of these walls. I *need* to talk to you. Tomorrow? Eastgate Park?'

She was already shaking her head before he had finished speaking. 'I don't know what you think is going on here, Jacob, but we are still up for the same job. I think we should keep things professional from here on in.'

'What?' Jacob said, clearly aghast.

He went to touch her arm, to guide her away somewhere, but she pulled her hand away—hard. 'Dr Peterson,' she said, and her professional, detached voice sounded alien even to her. 'I have work to do, and I'm sure you do too. Let's just forget everything else, okay?'

She took a few steps back, folding her arms and fixing him with a stare she struggled to hold. He looked so upset, so confused. *Why* was this man such a puzzle? When they'd been together the day before she had never felt so cherished, so desired, so *seen* by anyone before. He'd made her feel alive, made her want to share her life with him. She cared what he thought about her even now, and she hated herself for being so weak around him.

'Michelle, I don't understand…'

He took a step closer to her and her fight-orflight response kicked in. She pinched the skin around her left thumb-pad between her fingers, grabbing and twisting it till it seemed as if it was going to tear from her bones.

He saw and raised a hand. 'Michelle—stop. Look at me, okay? I'm here. I'm here for you, Mich.'

*I'm here for you.*

Those words. Of all the thousands of words in the world, they were too much.

Raising her head high, fixing Jacob with a hard look, she took the business card between her fingers and tore it in half, repeating the action till the card was a pile of paper confetti in her shaking fingers.

'I don't need anyone, Jacob. Have you not worked that out yet? I have my friends and my job. I had them before you, and I will have them after you've moved on to your next… challenge.' She turned her palm over, letting the pieces flutter to the floor. 'If you're feeling lonely from now on check your messages. I'm sure you'll find some company.'

She didn't hear his reply. She was already out of there—back to work. Jacob Peterson could jolly well please himself from now on. This job was what she needed, and she wasn't about to let it slip through her fingers like that business card of a total ding-dong.

She ignored the splintering pain in her heart as she strode away from the man she knew she was falling for.

'Michelle!' he called after her, and she closed her eyes against the sting of tears. 'What did I do? What messages?'

'Messages?' Jacob panted at the receptionist behind the desk. 'Messages...for...' He pointed at himself with a double thumb movement. He'd run all the way in a state of mild panic. 'I hear you have messages?'

The woman looked at him wide-eyed. 'I did, Doctor, but I put them in your pigeonhole.'

He nodded, still gasping for air, and half ran around the reception desk to the wall of staff pigeonholes. Thumbing through the pieces of paper, he frowned, brandishing them in his fist and waggling them at the poor woman.

'Is this all of them?' he asked, wondering what the hell was going on.

The woman winced, pointing down the corridor.

'I did give one of them to another doctor yesterday, to pass on to you. Was that wrong?'

She looked as if she was about to burst into tears and Jacob felt bad. He wasn't meaning to come across so bullish—he just needed to know what had changed Michelle's mind about him…what had turned her so cold. He'd tasted her now, and that couldn't be the last time. He wouldn't cope if it was.

He pushed the pieces of paper back into his pigeonhole and went over to the receptionist. 'I'm sorry…er…'

'Elaine.' The woman sniffed. 'I gave a message to Dr Forbes yesterday. I thought you were in the on-call room, but—'

Jacob's pager buzzed in his pocket and he checked it. Home—checking in. He read the message, feeling a second of relief. Ebony was fine and having a good day. She'd be heading to the park now with her nanny, if she hadn't already.

'Okay, so you gave it to Dr Forbes. What did it say?'

Elaine reached over her desk and grabbed a pink duplicate pad, flicking back through the entries to find her carbon copy of the message.

'Here we are,' she said shrilly.

She folded over the page and showed it to him in such a way that it told him she was by now terrified of him and his rather bizarre behaviour. To be fair, it was a little unlike him. He was the cool one—Mr Ice. Not lately, though. Not since Michelle had landed in his life.

Reading the notepad message, he felt his face drop.

*Jesus Christ.*

'She read this?' he checked.

Elaine nodded. 'She said she would pass it on…that you weren't there but she would be seeing you.'

Something clicked in Jacob's memory. Like a piece that didn't quite fit till you turned it round and looked at it from a new angle. She'd got this message while they'd been together in the on-call room.

'That's why she left,' he muttered under his breath bleakly.

'Is something wrong, Doctor?' Elaine asked, her hands knitted together in front of her.

He smiled, passing the pad back to her. His pager went off again. Home? 'No problem,

Elaine. Sorry for worrying you. It's my fault—nothing to worry about. Thank you.'

Elaine smiled, her panic subsiding. 'No problem, Doctor. Do you want to take your messages now?'

His pager went off again, and he waved Elaine away. 'No, thank you, Elaine, I'll grab them later. Next time only pass them to me, okay? Gotta go—trauma incoming!'

Half of his words were whipped into the air as he ran away from her to the ambulance doors.

His pager vibrated in his pocket again, and he saw Call home on the display.

Damn. He'd probably forgotten some trip slip or paperwork that needed signing for school, but he didn't have time now. Today was turning into a great day for annoying just about every female in his life, it seemed.

He winced at the thought and arrived at his destination to see a figure already there, briefing the trauma team while they gowned up in plastic aprons, gloves and headgear. Whatever it was, it clearly merited half the staff being here.

Michelle was gowned up too, and reading from a clipboard in her hand, using her pen to point people towards different areas to set up. He was almost at her side when she spotted him. A strange expression crossed her features for half a second, and then she was back to being Dr Forbes, trauma goddess. Tormentor of his very being.

'RTA, corner of St John's Road. School bus and a goods lorry. One confirmed fatality at the scene—the driver of the lorry. The other vehicles were a woman and a girl in a car—minor injuries. They were clipped by the bus as the truck hit it. They're on their way in. Second ambulance is still there. Some issue at the scene.'

She looked at him over her clipboard. People were flying in all directions around them, as the distant scream of sirens got nearer. Tannoy announcements echoed inside the walls, and people and equipment scrambled like a well-oiled machine.

For the pair of them the department might as well have been empty. They stood only inches apart, but a world away from each other. Jacob could see that she had deleted him from her memory, wiped out the few blissful moments they had enjoyed. He'd messed it all up, and he didn't know how to get out of it without causing further damage.

'How bad?' he asked.

'Bad,' she replied. 'Twelve kids are on their way in; the rest are being treated for cuts and shock at the scene, waiting for transfer here. We have the beds, thank God. No criticals yet, but the bus driver is still being cut out by the fire brigade.'

Jacob nodded, turning to face the throng of people in the trauma bay. 'Right, people. RTA incoming—three minutes! We need blood cross-checked and ready, we need blankets, bandages, and trauma trays set up for glass removal, cut-cleaning, stitching. Students—anyone mastered stitching, good suture techniques?'

A couple of hands went up from the pool of eager juniors who were hanging around in the corner of the department, hoping to get the chance to help.

He pointed at the two of them. 'You—go set up some suturing trays for the bays. Ask a nurse if you're not sure. You—number two—' he didn't have the time to look for a name tag or worry about hurt feelings here '—call Plastics. Get someone down here. They can assess the patients first, see what you can scoop up. Learn from them, people, and get moving!'

For a second nothing much happened, and Jacob noticed a few of the staff were looking at Michelle for direction. Too many cooks. *Goddamn it.* How could they work together if she hated him like this?

Michelle looked at Jacob and addressed the room. 'You heard the doctor! We run this trauma together—get moving, people!' She raised the clipboard towards the doors, like a warrior holding aloft a sword. 'Incoming—brace yourselves! No one else dies today, you hear me?'

*Boom.* Her words ignited the room, galvanising every person from the timid receptionist to the gaggle of student doctors who didn't know one end of a central line from the other. Everyone helped, everyone worked together, and Jacob and Michelle were like one entity, one brain.

The bus crash victims came in ones and twos, a fleet of ambulances bringing them through the doors. Their loved ones followed in tears, phones ringing in their bags and pockets. They came brandishing photos on their phone screens, gripping gilded silver photo frames they had ripped from sills and hearths and bed-side tables to help identify their child.

Jacob couldn't bring himself to look at them, at their pain and utter terror. He'd seen that look on too many faces. So he focused on the people he could help—the ones needing medical attention.

The lorry driver's wife arrived a short time later, to see her husband, and Jacob took that second to escape. He couldn't bear to look her in the face, to feel her pain. That woman's life would be altered for ever after she'd walked through those doors, and he hated that part of his job. Hated seeing the ones they were too late for…the ones who'd never had a chance… never even saw it coming.

Heading to the on-call room, he tried the bathroom door but found it locked.

'Sorry,' he said, cursing the intruder. Then he heard it—the soft sound of someone weeping. 'Hello? Who's in there?' He banged on the door once and it opened.

'I'm in here. I just needed a minute,' Michelle said gruffly, throwing a ball of rolled-up tissue into the wastepaper basket behind her and moving past him.

'You okay?' he asked, already knowing the answer.

Some shifts were much worse than others, and today was still happening.

'I'm okay.' She looked at him for the first time and her fingers flexed instinctively towards him at her sides, but she folded her arms, setting her face stubbornly.

'Me too,' he admitted. 'Did you see—?'

'The widow? Yeah, that's what set me off.'

Jacob's heart swelled. Here they were—not together, not even speaking, really—and they were so similar in so many ways.

He opened his mouth to tell her, but she beat him to it.

'I need you to leave me alone, Jacob. Please.'

She said it like *We need more pens in the nurses' station* or *Pass the butter.*

Jacob's words fell out of his head, jumbling into a pile in the pit of his stomach.

'I just need you to be my colleague today. The rest is done. Dead.'

* * *

*Why me? Why him? Did he follow me? Sense my presence somehow?*

When she'd opened the bathroom door to see him standing there, his lips tight with concern, she'd wanted to cry all over again, to run into his arms. But that wasn't her style. She'd needed a minute away from the pain and the sobs and the stricken faces of the relatives waiting for news of their loved ones, of their children—those same children they had kissed that morning before sending them off all excited for their school trip.

Sometimes life just seemed so unfair.

Before she'd known what was happening, she'd almost blurted out the words that had been rattling around in her head for months, never fully forming, always lurking silently. But she'd grabbed those words and pushed them kicking and screaming back into her mouth.

She wanted to get it out there—to tell someone. To tell *him*. Despite herself, and that damn pink note, she couldn't help but still feel the attraction between them. Their shorthand in the trauma department was perfect; they worked together like a pair of limbs, each one knowing where the other was at all times.

She hadn't had that since Rebecca, and that crushing thought was the one thing that threatened to break the dam. She couldn't let it, though—not now. She had to get away from him, and she wasn't strong enough to do it alone. He had to stay away, to give her a chance of getting past this. Over him.

'I know you're going through hell, but I can help. I'm a mess too, Mich. I need to tell you something, but you won't listen!'

'Be my colleague today. Can you do that?' she asked again. 'Can you just be my colleague?'

Jacob took one step closer and both their pagers went off. He groaned in frustration when he read his.

'The occupants of the car are two minutes out,' he said flatly.

Nodding, Michelle pulled an errant strand of hair away from her face and, brushing herself down, followed him as he ran to the ambulance bay.

Two ambulances were coming in, and Jacob waited for the second.

Michelle already had her hand on the door

of the first. The woman on the gurney was conscious, but very quiet, a wet slash of blood across her forehead and cheekbone. Michelle checked her pupils, working carefully around the collar.

'How long has she been like this?' she asked.

The paramedic, Waseela, looked at her watch a millisecond before answering. 'Less than three minutes. Her pupils are equal and responsive. She's in a state of shock. She was on her phone earlier, trying to contact someone, but she wasn't making a lot of sense. She has a broken arm from the collision; she was trying to shield the passenger with her arm.'

The second ambulance screeched to a halt and Michelle saw Jacob go for the doors from the corner of her eye. He was on the case, and it felt good to have him there, at her side, even with her question still unanswered and his evident frustration.

She returned to her patient, asking for some more details, checking her vision as they walked her in—but then something stopped her in her tracks. The girl in the other ambulance was awake, and in a state of distress.

'Get off me! Don't touch me! It hurts…it hurts!'

Jacob froze—just for a moment, but Michelle noticed, and passed her patient to a nurse and headed over to help.

'Daddy!' The little girl said. 'Daddy!'

She had a plaster on her forehead and the skin on her face was cut, tiny little slits where the glass from the side windows of the car must have shattered with the impact.

Jacob had jumped into the back of the ambulance, and before anyone could object he sat himself behind the little girl on the gurney, her back resting against his front, and he slowly and gently wrapped his arms around her. The little girl stopped shouting and started whimpering, rocking back and forth. He rocked with her, whispering softly into her ear, words of encouragement, of love.

The crew brought her out, wheeling her off to the bay. Michelle followed.

'Daddy, I rang you!' the little girl sobbed.

Michelle looked around, but no one seemed to be racing to the youngster's side. Moving away a little, she beckoned to Jude, who was just updating the emergency board.

'Jude, can we call the family for this little girl? The driver she's with doesn't look as though she's the mother. Grandmother, maybe? I want to get her admitted, but Jacob's taken the lead.'

Looking back at the pair, she saw Jacob rubbing the girl's back while he held her tight on the gurney. The staff were keeping their distance from them and rushing to help other patients. Something felt odd. Jacob was good with kids, sure—she'd already seen that—but why wasn't he moving?

'Have a word, Jude, and get her details. I'll go and see to the driver.'

Michelle looked from the nurse to Jacob, and to the girl. She looked so familiar...

'Daddy, who's the lady?' a little voice asked, and Jacob's eyes flicked to where Michelle was standing, watching from the curtained doorway to a cubicle. He gave her an apologetic half-smile.

Softly, he spoke. 'I'm sorry. The park date was going to be an introduction.'

*The park date she had refused to go on.*

He looked at her with his big green eyes and it clicked in her head.

'I did try to tell you. This is my daughter.'

He turned back to the little girl while Michelle looked on. She'd seen her before—around the hospital, in the cafeteria, the gift shop. She was always with an older woman. She just looked like any other visitor—aside from the headphones and chewable jewellery.

The little girl with the juice… She'd spoken to her, said hi in the corridor, a few times since. The happy, polite little girl who had stolen her heart that day was his *daughter*. He'd not been hiding her, just biding his time, and she'd shut him down at every single opportunity.

'This is Daddy's friend, honey—Dr Forbes. She's here to make you all better.'

The little girl looked at her father with wide eyes that were a carbon copy of his own. Michelle saw it then. It was obvious. She was a mini-version of him—the same dark lashes, the eyes ever-searching, the bow of her lips, the turn of her cute little nose.

Him—all him.

*He has a daughter?*

Something else clicked in her—snippets of conversation they had shared over the weeks they had spent together.

*'I have to tell you something.'*

He'd tried to tell her. That had to be it.

'And Susan, too?' The little girl with dark brown hair, matted a little now from the accident, looked right at Michelle. 'Will you make my nanny better too? She fell asleep.'

The driver in shock was his daughter's nanny. The poor child must have been terrified.

Looking at Jacob's pale face, she could see that he was pretty shaken too, and her crushed heart still felt for him. Jacob Peterson: playboy doctor, player, battle-scarred hero… Father?

She was giving herself a headache, trying to make the pieces fit. There'd been more than love and rivalry between them in the on-call room. There had been secrets too—and not just the ones *she* kept. The women, the bravado, the tours—all with a daughter in tow? She couldn't reconcile the old parts of him with the new. It didn't make sense.

'Dr Forbes?'

A nurse from Orthopaedics sidled up to her, chart in hand. Michelle could have kissed her for providing a distraction when she needed one.

'The driver of the car is back with you. She's

had her scans done and a half-slab put on till the swelling goes down. Jude is with her now.'

'Thank you, Nurse.' She pinned her face into an easy smile, despatching her and turning back to Jacob and the child. 'Lovely to meet you, Miss Peterson,' she said kindly, giving the girl a genuine smile.

The little girl didn't return it at first, but slowly a little smile crept across her features.

'I have a patient, but I'll be back soon.'

'But—'

She heard Jacob start to talk to her, but she wanted to be nowhere near either of them right now.

She checked on the driver; the woman was indeed the girl's nanny, but that was all they knew. As well as the broken arm she has a lot of soreness to contend with, so the last thing she needed was the staff who were meant to be caring for her asking inappropriate questions about her employer.

Michelle got back to work, checking each patient over, double and triple-checking everything. At one point, charting in one of the side rooms, she snapped a pencil in half with her hand. Her grip had been too tight and the pressure of her worry and anxiety had been too much to bear.

She needed help, and she needed it now.

The third floor welcomed her once more like a soft pink bubble. The carpet seemed to bounce underfoot when she hit the corridor and nodded to the receptionist. Today, after the bus crash trauma, she was glad that she had prebooked this slot, and now she had something else to talk about: the fact that she was falling for her work rival—the man who was currently downstairs comforting his surprise child and no doubt waiting for her anguished and stunningly beautiful mother.

It was another complication to their lives, and they weren't even together. She thought she'd felt low when she saw that note, but now this—a child? It was too much even to try to wrap her head around. Surely even the strongest women in the world needed a bit of help from time to time. Sometimes a good push-up bra and a can-do attitude with a side of denial wouldn't cut the mustard.

The buzzer sounded the second after she sat down on the waiting couch, or so it felt. Nodding to the receptionist, she walked into the consulting room on shaky legs, not daring to look up till she was safely sitting down on the familiar leather chair.

Greg was in his usual seat, his manner gentle and calm as always. Michelle tucked her hands on her lap, the thumb and forefinger of one hand pinching and nipping at the thumb-pad of the other. They both looked at the clock—a matter of habit—and when the time signalled the top of the hour Greg clicked his pen.

'So, Michelle,' he said, 'where shall we start?'

The little girl in his arms sagged, and Jacob knew she had finally given in to her fatigue and fallen asleep. He moved as quickly and as smoothly as he could, placing her gently into bed and watching her sleep. She looked so pale and drawn Jacob couldn't stand it. He walked backwards out of the cubicle, heading to the nurses' station.

Jude was at the computer, and her look told him that people around here hadn't missed a trick.

'Yes, she's my daughter,' he said. 'The nanny was taking her out for the day. Is Susan okay?'

Jude pursed her lips, nodding. 'She's sleeping; her family is on the way.'

Jacob sighed, feeling guilty that one of his first thoughts was that he had no childcare, and no idea how to sort that out before it affected his job. But the whole accident could have been a hell of a lot worse, and he knew it, which made his thoughts seem all the more selfish.

'That's good. Page me when they get here? I'm going to stay tonight anyway.'

Jude nodded, her icy demeanour thawing just a fraction. 'No problem. Need a bed making up?'

He shook his head. 'I'll do it when I get back. I just want to go and get some things from home. Did they bring their belongings from the car?'

Jude nodded, pointing back to where his daughter was sleeping. 'I put her bag in her locker. Your nanny packs well.'

Jacob smiled, thinking of the bag of magic that was sitting in that wooden locker. 'She sure does. Thanks, Jude. Dr Forbes around?'

'She had an appointment,' the nurse told him. 'You could have told us, you know…about your daughter. We would have helped.'

'I was new in the job, Jude, and the single dad thing is rather new to me. I was going to tell people, but then—'

'But then Michelle came back and it got complicated.'

Jude's arched brow reminded him just how observant and astute nurses were.

'Got it in one. I *do* care, you know—about her. About both of them…'

Jude was already focused back on her screen now, and she didn't answer. Girl code or busy professional?

A bit of both, he thought wryly.

It spoke a lot about how loved Michelle was that people cared so much, closed ranks even against him, a superior. If only they knew how strongly he felt that protective instinct too—felt that fire in his belly that made him want to run to her, to seek her out.

They didn't need to shelter Michelle from him. He'd take a bullet to spare her an ounce of pain. She made him better just by being in his life. He had a passion for her, for the job, for life again, and now he'd gone and blown the lot apart.

What was it she had said before? *'Leave me alone. Please.'*

Just recalling her words made his gut drop to the soles of his shoes.

'Jude, where *is* Dr Forbes?' He changed his voice, back to the commanding professional.

Jude looked at him, jaw tight. 'She's off the trauma floor for a while; she won't be much longer.'

She gave him a sarky little smile and returned to tapping the keys—this time a little harder. She no doubt expected him to slink off, but he stayed firm.

'Well, page her, please. Call her back to the floor.'

He needed to see her *now*—had to. He had to explain, find out what was wrong.

Had she left the hospital? Who was she meeting ?

Jude huffed and, picking up the phone, sent a page out. Replacing the receiver, she nodded to him in a *I did it, now leave me alone* way and returned to her typing.

The page went unanswered, and Jacob grew more and more frustrated. He glanced back at the cubicle, checking his daughter was still fast asleep, and then turned to walk away, pulling his car keys out of his pocket.

'Keep paging her till she answers; tell her I need to see her urgently. I'll be back soon.'

Jude barely acknowledged him and he narrowed his eyes at her, feeling his tongue loosening with stress.

'Jude, I do need to speak to Dr Forbes. It is important, and I expect you to do your job.'

She looked at him lazily over the top of her monitor. His threat hadn't even hit the board, let alone the bullseye.

'I am doing my job, Dr Peterson,' she said pointedly. 'My boss is off the floor, and will answer your page when she gets back, I'm sure. Anything else?'

She raised a brow at him, and he didn't know whether to report her to Andrew or to laugh.

The clock had kept on ticking all the same, even after she'd opened her mouth to speak and uttered those words to Greg. Three little words, she'd said to him, and then three little words she hadn't uttered to Jacob.

*Rebecca is dead. Jacob's a father.*

She had been watching the clock the whole

time while she spoke, the fingers of her left hand pinching the inner skin of her opposite forearm distractedly, twisting it to the point of pain because that felt less painful than the words she was pushing out of her mouth.

She'd said the words and the clock had ignored them. No reaction, no stalling. The machinery had kept going, the mechanism free of guilt and loss, free of pain.

*Whatever happens in this room, the clock never stops ticking.*

The thought entered her head and she focused on it, grabbing on to it and marvelling that life could be so cruel and so bleak and no one truly acknowledged it.

Why did they even bother? Right now she would rather be a ticking clock. Machinery without emotion.

'Does it bother you?' Greg asked, and she realised that she had spoken out loud. 'The clock?'

She looked at the clock face again and nodded. He'd asked her to focus on her first three words.

'I hate it that Rebecca doesn't get to move on like the clock—to live like we do.'

She thought of Kathryn then—Rebecca's mother. She was still carrying on, still surviving. She was doing better than Michelle was, and she couldn't imagine what strength that took. If *she* had lost a daughter, would she still be here? Would she still be on this earth at all?

She thought of Jacob then, his pale, terrified face as he'd scrambled to comfort his daughter, to wrap her in his strong arms. She knew how it felt to be held like that, and she wanted to go to him—but how could she?

Everything was so linked together and such a mess. Jacob had slept with Becks and now she was dead, and now he was here, with a secret family in tow. A family he must have had back then. Had Becks known and not cared? It was all a mess, a jumble of faces and pain in her head, and she couldn't stand it.

'I hate it that Jacob knew her, had a history with her. It's all so entwined together—and that's before I knew about his child.'

Greg's eyebrows rose, which for him was a reaction. 'You hate that they had each other, or that he had a daughter back home?'

'Both,' she spat. 'I can't un-jumble them in my head. Everything is just so…so…'

'Linked?' Greg offered, and Michelle found herself nodding. 'But we are *all* linked, Michelle. Karinthy talked about six degrees of separation, and I often see things like this occurring with my patients. Have you spoken to Jacob since?'

Michelle shook her head. 'He was with his daughter; it wasn't the time. I'm not sure he even took in what I was saying. I needed him to leave me be so I wouldn't tell him how I felt. Feel.'

She hoped he hadn't heard her at all. It didn't matter now. It was over, anyway, and she didn't want him to have ammunition against her for taking the job. She had to focus on the job now—that was what she needed to stay afloat. To be here and work, to talk to Greg, to try to get out from the deep fog in which she was constantly immersed.

She needed fifty degrees of separation, not six. She needed Jacob to leave so she could burrow into the hospital and hole up for the dark winter she was facing in her mind.

The worst part was, now she would have to bear the loss of him too.

'You have to process the events yourself if

you have any hope of sharing your pain with others,' said Greg. 'I think it's time. This is the low point, Michelle; you can see the bottom. Let's start to look up. This is the time—right now.'

Michelle looked at him, digging into her skin even harder with her nails. Greg gazed at her clasped hands, expressionless, and she sat back on the couch, tucking her hands underneath her to stop herself.

'I don't know if I can,' she admitted, already fighting against the emotions she had suppressed for so long.

Greg thought for a moment and then went to get something from his desk drawer. Coming back to his chair, he passed her a small pile of elastic bands, putting one around his wrist and snapping it lightly against his skin.

'Let's try this and take it slow. We can stop whenever you want.' He sat back in his chair, adopting his usual open posture. 'You ready? Tell me about that day, Michelle. What do you remember about it?'

Michelle winced as an image of Becks on the ground screamed in her head.

'I can't.' She twanged a band against her own

wrist and felt a flash of relief from the pain in her chest. All too soon, though, it was gone. 'I can't speak to you about this. I can't speak to anyone.'

'Anyone?' Greg said softly, kindly. 'There's no one in your life that you could share this with? Just telling someone is enough, Michelle. It's a start. You need to start talking about this—start letting people in. You can't do everything alone and you shouldn't have to.'

Michelle looked at him. 'And how do I do that, exactly? Let people in?'

He looked at her for a moment, before looking back at the ticking clock.

'One day at a time, Michelle. That's how. Next time we'll talk more.'

Jacob pulled into the car park with a back seat full of clothes and a rather ugly green crocodile. It was his daughter's favourite toy—the one that she'd drooled on as a baby and still wanted when she was scared or tired. She'd been so wiped out she had managed to fall asleep without it, but he wanted to see her face light up when she saw Crocky.

Or Crocky Six, he should say, since he had

a closet full of the stuffed toys as back-ups. He'd caught on fast after Crocky One had met an ugly demise under the wheels of a street sweeper. He could still remember the cloud of fluff as poor original Crocky had been lost against the might of those powerful brushes. His daughter's heartbroken cries. Jenny's growing frustration with her daughter. It had been a sign of how things would end for them.

He grabbed Ebony's things, with his own overnight bag, and headed inside. After checking on his daughter and her nanny, and finding them both settled and asleep for the night, he took one look at the put-up bed in the corner of Ebony's room and walked the other way.

There was no chance of sleep—not yet. He needed to walk it off. His pager was quiet, and Jude had left for the day. He didn't have the heart to ask the other nurses to keep paging Michelle. If she'd wanted to answer him, she would have. It was too late.

The chapel was a hidden oasis of calm in a tucked-away corner of the hospital, with dark wooden pews and a large altar at the front, a metal candle rack for votive candles to one side.

There were always candles lit, shining out to remember someone lost or to pray for someone hovering between life and death. It smelled of sandalwood and candle wax, the scent of a holy place, and there was a waft of lavender as she passed vases full of small bundles.

In whatever corner of the world a bolthole like this could be found, they all held the same reverent air, gave people the same sense of being in the presence of something far bigger than their problems. Michelle was far from re-ligious, but she wanted to be alone and this had seemed as good a place as any.

She headed down the empty aisle, past the vacant pews, till she reached the front and felt the warmth from the candles. Taking a fresh one from the wooden box on an adjacent table, she lit it and placed it at the front. Watching the flame flicker, she heard a swish of the doors behind her, and turned around to see Jacob standing there.

'I've been looking for you,' he said, looking at her pager, clearly visible and hanging from her belt clip. 'You okay?'

He took a step forward and she shook her head, stopping him in his tracks.

'No, not really. You?'

Jacob walked slowly towards her, his easy gait gone, his body tense and coiled. He was stressed, she realised, and she thought of his daughter—the little girl she'd been saying hello to for weeks.

'Has your wife arrived yet?'

She wanted to tell him how angry she was, how stupid she felt. How devastated she was that he wasn't free when she wanted him for her own, despite everything in her telling her to run.

A daughter wasn't a deal-breaker—far from it. Being the other woman was.

She wanted him to smart from her words, to feel the brunt of her disappointment and pain.

'I don't have a wife,' he said, his eyes fixed on hers, his feet moving slowly towards her, always moving. 'Or a girlfriend. Currently.'

'Ah, baby mama, then,' Michelle quipped, wondering why he was still coming towards her. She wanted to tell him to stop as much as she wanted to run into his arms and bawl like a baby. 'How very modern of you.'

His step faltered and he didn't take the next one. It was working. The grenades she was throwing at him were slowing him down. She wanted him to hurt like she did, and she couldn't stop the words coming from her mouth.

'I was engaged once. To Ebony's mother.'

*Ebony. The note.*

'The note was from your daughter?' she asked, giving herself away. 'The message?'

He nodded sheepishly. 'I'm a single dad, Mich, not a player. Maybe once upon a time… sure. But I was single then. We did try to stay together, but we both knew it was a mistake. We called off the engagement before the ink on the ring receipt had dried. We shared custody for a while, but it didn't go well. Ebony has autism, and Jenny wasn't able to cope. She did her best on her own, while I was working abroad, but then she got a new partner and things didn't go well. Ebony wasn't happy, and her health started to suffer. Jenny asked me to take over, so I came home and took Ebony with me. I hired a nanny, bought a house, and got the job here. I should have told you, Michelle, but I didn't know how. With everything else… and you. I never expected to meet you. I never expected to meet anyone like you.'

He stopped and smiled then, taking three

steps towards her as though he just couldn't help himself.

'I didn't expect you. I know you hate me, but...'

'I don't hate you,' she said, going to sit down on the front pew and resting her head on the wooden back of the low seat. 'I've tried, believe me. I need you.'

She felt the low rumble of his laughter as he sat down near her, leaving a small gap between them.

'I've tried to hate you too, but I don't,' he said, his beautiful full lips curling into a half-smile. 'I like hearing that you need me, though. I feel the same. Do you want to tell me about what else is going on with you?'

She noted how he was careful not to push.

'What happened?' he asked.

She bit her lip till it hurt, then remembered the rubber band round her wrist and switched to that instead.

'I need to talk to someone. My therapist tells me it's the next step. But...'

*Pain. Screams. Debris. Dust. Blades. Gunfire. Shouting. Running. The sound of my own blood pumping around my body.*

She closed her eyes, her hand grabbing at the skin on her thigh.

Jacob's voice punched through the terrifying montage in her head, his words permeating her brain. 'I'm here, Michelle. It's okay. Talk to me.'

She reached for the elastic band, pulling it back and snapping it hard. She felt a sharp sting on the skin of her wrist and did it again. And again.

She looked at him, and mentally steeled herself. She was here, with him. Present. And her heart soared.

'Now, slowly, Michelle. Take it slow. Tell me.'

A flash of her friend's hair, matted with blood and dust, made her wince as though she had been stabbed in the side.

'I can't,' she said, her eyes welling up. 'I can't. I won't. It's too bad.'

'You can,' Jacob said, firm, confident, guiding. 'Tell me what you need to.'

She thought hard, her eyes still closed. She twanged the band again and then she was back there…on her old bunk. Transported into the memory as though it were tangible. The camp was quiet, the chaos something yet to occur.

Rebecca was lying on her bunk, stitching a piece of orange cloth and laughing at Michelle.

'It's not like that! I'm not getting *married* to the man; it's just sex.'

Michelle had wrinkled her nose in disgust, making her friend laugh all the more.

'Give up being such a priss and making me laugh! I nearly stabbed myself with the needle.'

Michelle had thrown a sweet in her direction. Becks had caught it in her mouth with flair.

'I'm not a priss!' Michelle had said. 'I just don't see the point, to be honest. When are you ever going to see him again and why would you want to? Isn't he a player?'

Becks had snorted. 'Calm down, Jane Austen. I have no need or want of a husband, thank you. I just need to get laid and do my job. He's *fun*! It's no strings and he brings me pudding after—I mean, who wouldn't want pudding *and* dessert?'

She'd waggled her brows at Michelle, making her crack her sour face into a smile.

'He has his life, his own stuff going on back home, and I have you and my work. You don't fulfil *all* my needs, you know. You dragged me on this tour, but you didn't give me any toys to play with.'

She'd finished off her stitch, cutting the thread short and throwing the material at Michelle. Michelle had caught it and smiled.

'Sometimes you just need someone to hold you close and make you feel alive, like a woman should. He does that. We have fun. End of.'

'End *away*, more like.'

Michelle had tried and failed to be cross. She had known there was nothing wrong with a bit of fun. She had known she needed to lighten up.

A bit of company wouldn't go amiss for herself, if she was being honest, she'd thought. Scott had come to mind, and she'd realised that, although she missed him, she was dreading the next time they met. He'd been so cold on the phone last time they had managed to speak.

She'd unfolded the orange material and seen the delicate stitching, her initials stitched under the edge of one of the corners.

'A scrubs cap? This is gorgeous!' Michelle had put the hat on her head, tying it closed. It had fitted perfectly. 'For me?'

She'd looked back at her friend, who had been wearing an identical one, dying to laugh.

They'd both laughed for ages, dubbing themselves the scrubs cap twins, and had stayed up later than they should have, talking, but they hadn't cared. Those were the moments that kept them going when the firing started and the casualties started rolling in.

'That was our last night together,' Michelle said, finally holding up her head and looking Jacob in the eye. 'It happened the day after, and then she was gone. It was my fault, don't you see? I was right there. I tried to save her, but she died right in front of me.'

Jacob's eyes crinkled at the corners, but he kept his composure. 'Michelle, I read the reports. There was an ambush—a rebel band. You couldn't have foreseen that; no one could. Army personnel had no intel to suggest that your medical camp was under threat, and you two staying up a little late didn't cause any of that. You have survivor guilt, Michelle, and I suspect PTSD. It's important that you listen to me when I say this. It's not your fault, Michelle.'

She snapped the band on her wrist.

*One. Two. It's not your fault. Three. Four. It's not your fault.*

'Your friend died, and you were there with her at the end. You comforted her, you had her back, and you never left her side. Even when the world was falling down around you. You didn't panic, and you didn't make a false step or a wrong move. You saved people in a war zone and your friend didn't die alone. She left this life with you right there, showing her the love you showed her throughout your time together. You did nothing wrong, Michelle, and you need to stop feeling guilty for living. You need to say goodbye.'

Jacob pulled her into his side, hushing her cries and kissing her tears.

'I'm sorry… I had no idea… I came back home for Ebony. The news coming out of camp was sketchy, at best, and I couldn't go back. I had to ground myself. But I'm here now, Mich. Say your goodbyes. We're here, in this chapel. Speak to her.'

She snapped her band methodically, and slowly, very slowly, started to talk.

She spoke to Jacob and she spoke to Becks. Him being there felt strange, but also…*right*.

She found herself telling him everything. How Becks had died, how lost she'd felt since. How the job, and then him, were the only things keeping her going. How she had been feeling so guilty, and how he had unknowingly helped her to work through things, challenging her and making her *feel* once more.

'So...' Jacob said eventually, when she had fallen silent. 'Do you think it helped?'

He was holding her hand tight in his, resting it on his lap. He was stroking her thumb slowly, tenderly, and the look he was giving her wasn't pity, but...

She didn't want to say it.

They were both such a mess, and in a few short days they would be in front of Andrew, fighting for a job that they both desperately needed. It wasn't a situation that Michelle could see any way out of, and she didn't want to think about it any more. She had done enough for today. She had exorcised as many demons as she could.

And as they both gazed at each other, happy in their silence, she couldn't help but think that without him she wouldn't have come this far. Not that she would tell him that...

# CHAPTER EIGHT

'WHO WANTS PUDDING?' Jacob asked jovially, heading towards Ebony's room with a pack of her favourite chocolate dessert pots. He passed Wendy and waggled them at her. 'Wendy, do you fancy a teatime snack?'

He snapped one of the pots from its plastic housing and thrust it in the nurse's direction.

Wendy grinned and put it in her pocket. 'Thanks, Dr Peterson! Cute daughter, by the way.' She saluted him, heading off down the ward corridor, a spring in her step now.

The whole mood of the place had improved today. Michelle was working with Jacob on a double, and he was overjoyed to have twelve whole hours of working alongside her.

Andrew had grown noticeably more and more quiet as the time neared for the grand opening of the new trauma centre, and Jacob knew the decorators were scheduled to arrive in a day's time to start the cosmetic finessing. It was getting down to the wire now, but Jacob didn't find himself eager to get all the big cases today, to get himself noticed. He was, for once, just living in the moment.

'Dad, don't give all my pudding away!'

Ebony often acted as though she was twenty-seven years old, despite being only five, and when he walked into the room she was giving him her 'schoolmarm' look of reproach.

'Save some for Michelle!'

Jacob did a double-take as he clocked who was sitting in the chair by Ebony's bed. He saw Michelle tense, just for a second, and he gave her an easy smile. One that was appropriate in front of his only child and lacking his usual panty-dropping smoulder.

'I won't. I have plenty left for my favourite girls.'

Now it was Ebony's turn to beam at him. 'Daddy! Michelle's not a girl, she's a *lady*.'

'And I'm his boss.' Michelle winked at Ebony, making her giggle.

In such a short space of time she sure had won Ebony over fast, he thought. That girl didn't miss a trick, and she wasn't shy about speaking her mind either. Which probably meant they were two peas in a pod.

'Did you bring spoons, minion?' Michelle asked, standing up from the chair and coming to take the pudding pots from him.

Jacob waggled his hips at her as though he was trying to hula-hoop. 'Right here in my pocket.'

She smirked a little, seeing the plastic cutlery sticking out of his trousers and pulling them out with a flourish that made him go a little weak at the knees.

She skipped back over to Ebony's side, offering her a spoon and a pot of mousse. Ebony took them straight from her and Jacob's heart flipped. Ebony had issues with touch, as half the staff had found out when she'd been admitted. She didn't like to be touched by strangers, and yet taking that spoon from Michelle had looked as easy as breathing to Ebony. He found himself a little choked up and didn't trust himself to speak.

The two females in his new life ripped the tops off their sweet treats and giggled together as they tucked in. Jacob wanted to get his phone out and take a photo, to remember this moment.

He wanted the three of them to stay in this little bubble, away from jobs and battlefields and misunderstandings.

Looking at Michelle, who seemed brighter than he had ever seen her, he knew that she was feeling the same emotions.

*Maybe it's not too late after all. Maybe I can still keep her for ever.*

Ebony looked brighter today, and oddly relaxed around Michelle. What *was* it about her that put people at ease? He'd felt it as he'd watched her over the last few weeks—seeing how she dealt with patients and staff with the same care and respect. When no one was watching she even did some of the nurses' jobs—the ones that other doctors would never consider. She made this place feel like home— to the staff, to him. How could he go against her for the job with everything that had happened? He didn't want to think about it.

'You finished for the day?' Michelle asked him, licking her spoon clean and putting the empty pot down.

Ebony was just finishing hers and she eyed the two of them silently. She was a watcher, his girl. She didn't speak a hell of a lot but, boy, she never missed a trick. His daughter was as smart as a whip, and the way she was looking cautiously from face to face told him that she was picking up on every detail between them.

It made his stomach knot, to think that he might be bringing someone new into their family. Would she cope? Her mother was still in touch, but Jacob knew it was just a courtesy, really. He'd never even thought about the maternal instincts of the women he had slept with. But by the time he'd realised that he and Jenny were wholly unsuitable for each other, even as horizontal bed buddies, Ebony had been on the way and the die had been cast.

He felt two sets of eyes on him and shook himself out of his mood. 'I am. I was going to stay over, though, play a few games. Sound good, munchkin?'

Ebony wrinkled her nose at him, hiding her face a little. Michelle beckoned him, and he found himself kneeling before her. Ebony was already engrossed in the television that hung over the bed, mounted on a portable bracket, which was showing a wildlife programme.

'The other children are watching a film in the playroom after dinner,' Michelle told him. 'Ebony has signed up already.'

*Wow*, he thought to himself. *Ebony must feel comfortable here.*

Michelle must have caught his thought process, as she reached out and laid her hand on his, where it rested on the bed sheets. 'Jude's on later—she'll sit with them. She loves movie time; it's her thing.'

Jacob was nodding, willing himself to relax. She squeezed his hand again, and once more he wondered how she always seemed to be there for him, in his corner, and seemingly in Ebony's now too.

'Don't stress, Jacob, you look like the Hulk when you worry.' She made an over-exaggerated angry face, showing it to Ebony and making her laugh.

To Jacob's amazement, Ebony copied it, adding her own body-builder pose as she flexed imaginary green muscles at them both.

'Hulk smash!' she shouted, tittering into her little clenched fists.

Michelle giggled, holding up a hand that Ebony high-fived.

The sound of his daughter's laughter filled the room, and he closed his eyes, just for a split second, to capture the soundbite in his head for ever. He knew now, no matter what, that he had made the right decision. Wheels down was the way to go—and, looking at his daughter, safe and happy after the events of the last few months, he realised that it was enough.

He just needed a couple more pieces of the jigsaw to fit, and that would be plenty for him. He would choose the sound of his daughter being happy over any siren, any scramble, over the sounds of chopper blades in the desert. He was done, and for the first time he wanted to be at home. A home that had both of them in it.

A couple of hours later he said goodnight to Ebony, watching her get wheeled into the TV room, sweets and drinks in her little excited hands, and then nodded to Jude, who gave him a mock salute and waved him away. Ebony didn't even look back, but he waved her off till the doors closed and the sounds of the hospital filled his senses once more.

Leaning against the corridor wall, he ran

his hands down his face, trying to wake himself up.

'You going home?'

The voice to the side of him made him start. Andrew was walking up the corridor, his tie hanging from his partly open shirt, briefcase dangling from one hand.

'I was hoping to catch you, if you have the time?'

Jacob couldn't help but sigh, and Andrew winced.

'I know... I know. You've had it hard. It's just that we're less than two weeks from the new trauma centre opening, and both my star doctors are off their game.' He flicked his head in the direction of the TV room. 'How's your daughter and the nanny?'

He leaned against the wall too so they looked like a couple of sexy bookends to brighten up the stark white corridors.

'Fine,' Jacob replied, smiling at the relief he felt every time he thought of how lucky they had been. How much worse it could have been. 'Ebony can go home tomorrow, all being well, and her nanny is already home with her family. I don't think she'll be back any time soon, though; recovery will be a while with her injuries. No driving or working. Which means—'

'Which means,' Andrew said, preventing him from speaking any further with a nudge of his briefcase, 'that you need time. I get that. It's fine. But we need to make a plan, and soon. I have the refurbishment and rebranding of the trauma department to oversee, and I need a strong team. Have you and Michelle buried your issues?'

If only he knew. She'd buried *him*, truth be told. Planted him straight in a garden of lust and watched him grow into a song-singing, picket-fence-admiring man in love.

'We're rubbing along a little better,' he said. 'Has she left for the night?'

Andrew shrugged. 'I paged her, wanted the same talk with her, but I didn't get a reply. She's off-shift, so I'll catch up with her tomorrow. You get some rest, come see me tomorrow too. Even better, bring Michelle with you. We can make a plan together.'

*You took the words right out of my mouth.*

Jacob patted his boss on the shoulder, glad that Andrew had given him an out. He had plans, ideas, but every time he tried to put them to paper he stalled.

'I'll get my thinking cap on, Andrew. Good-night.'

He was halfway down the corridor when Andrew's voice reached his ears.

'Whatever happens, Jacob, on the day I *will* have a trauma chief, ready to go. Trauma waits for no one, and I can't hold this back.'

Jacob, not even turning around, gave Andrew a thumbs-up. 'Not a problem, boss. One trauma centre god, coming right up.'

Scribbling away on her notepad, Michelle squinted her eyes, closing them against the small shaft of bright artificial light that had suddenly danced across her bed. The on-call room door closed again, leaving her in near darkness. The only light in the room now was a slit from the street lamp outside, casting lines across her paper. She was in bed, the covers wrapped loosely around her as she lay on her tummy, writing a long overdue letter.

She was about to ask whoever it was that had come in not to turn the light on when the bathroom light went on and she saw Jacob. He looked exhausted, the lines under his eyes even darker in the shadows of the room.

She wanted to speak, but what could she say? Would anything come out right? They were skirting around each other. She was watching him, hidden underneath her blanket like a child scared of a storm.

He was like a tempest, of sorts. He had come into her workplace, whipped everything up, damaged and broken apart her perfect existence. He had shown her what her lies and unspoken words had done to her seemingly idyllic life. He'd made her hold a mirror up to herself and her problems, just as she had his—or so she hoped.

But maybe his daughter had that honour. Maybe, Becks had been right about him. He had just about smashed every assumption she had made about him, and watching him with his daughter…so tender, so patient. She had seen love, fatherly love and concern, and it had made her fall for him all the more.

'Hi,' she said, finding her voice.

It pierced the silence of the room and he turned his head, his eyes finding hers in the dark.

'Hey, you,' he said back. 'You writing my reference?'

She laughed at his attempt to break the ice. They were both feeling the pressure of the upcoming opening, and it made her feel oddly better that he was struggling with it too.

'Nope. I've already written, *Don't employ this moronic imbecile*. That didn't take long, so I decided to work on the rotas.' She held the paperwork aloft, and Jacob kicked open the bathroom door to let in more light. 'You can check it, if you like.'

Jacob slowly slid the page from her fingers, touching it gently. Michelle rolled over, looking up at the ceiling as he came to sit beside her, his eyes focused on the page.

It was early evening outside. An occasional laugh or cough could be heard outside in the corridor, and the odd trolley trundling past. He read it for days, it seemed, before placing it back on the bed next to her.

'Fine with me. You know, this might be the most awkward thing I have ever said to a woman I've slept with, but I really did like your friend Becks. She was a really nice person and I can tell you were really important to each other. I'm so sorry it happened.'

'Me too,' she echoed.

After her sessions with Greg she'd come to the slow realisation that he was right. They all were. What had happened to Becks had been catastrophic, but not her fault.

'Losing my best friend like that... I just felt so desperately useless. She was right there in front of me. I couldn't do a thing but watch her die. I think I died too, a little. And I got so angry I shut everyone out. Her mum has tried to reach out to me so many times since the funeral, and I've just batted her away. I'm selfish, Jacob.'

She was already playing with her hands, pinching and nipping, twisting the skin on her wrist. The elastic band had broken an hour back and lay on the carpeted floor.

Jacob reached into his pocket and wrapped something around her wrist. 'Here...'

He raised her hand and kissed it, just once, on the back. His lips felt like warm velvet on her skin. She felt the new elastic band tickle as it brushed across her bare wrist and she smiled.

'Just happen to have one in your pocket, eh?'

His other hand reached back into his pocket, pulling out a small pile of different coloured elastic bands.

'Norma from General Office hooked me up. I had to bring her chocolate muffins, though.'

He put them back into his pocket, sitting down on the bed alongside her. Their hands found each other again; she was eager for his touch.

'Do they help?' he asked.

She paused long enough to make him concerned, but then slowly nodded her head.

'They do, actually. I like the green.'

She ran her finger along the band, flashing him her happy smile—one that he seldom saw but worked all the harder to get each day. It was a personal challenge to him now, to see that expression on her face. The one that told him she was healing and getting stronger each day. God help them all at St Marshalls when she was fully recovered. She ran rings around them all on her worst day.

'How's Ebony?'

He grinned at the mention of his daughter's

name and lay back on the bed, taking Michelle's hand and her with him till they were lying side by side on the mattress.

'She's good. She likes you.'

He felt her shrug her shoulders beside him.

'She's gorgeous. I like her too.'

From her words, he could tell she was smiling.

'What are you going to do about childcare when she goes home?'

'That's pretty much all I've thought about, to be honest.'

*Besides obsessing about you, wanting to help you, mooning over you...*

'The agency has another nanny lined up; Ebony's due to meet her tomorrow, to see how they get on.'

Michelle didn't answer, and he squeezed her hand.

A fraction of a second later, she squeezed back.

'Andrew is getting pretty excited about the opening,' she said softly. 'He sent me an email today, with a dozen terrifying new names for the centre. He thinks we need to rebrand totally. He thinks it will help with the investors, who are apparently very impressed with his new drink-slinging and helicopter-hopping pair of doctors.'

Jacob laughed softly, turning on his side to face her. 'That was a pretty fun night.'

She laughed too, turning her head slightly to look him in the eye. 'I suppose it was, in the end. We *do* make a good team—when you listen to your boss.'

Jacob gasped theatrically, dropping her hands and tickling her. She squirmed and squealed, trying to get away from him.

'Okay, okay—I was joking!'

The single bed's frame kept her from getting away, and Jacob wasn't about to let her slip through his fingers.

'Stop, Jacob!'

He released her immediately, holding up his hands in surrender. Her eyes sparkled as she rose and hovered over him, her hands ready to tickle him back.

'Nope!' he said, taking the opportunity to wrap his leg over hers, pinning her to the bed.

She looked up at him, *so* sexy, and he couldn't take it any more.

'I think I'm falling, Michelle,' he said, wholly

unable to stop the words from coming out of his mouth. 'I know that's scary, but I really do like you.'

Seeing her with his daughter today had been the icing on the cake. The first time he had laid eyes on her he'd thought her a threat—a danger to his precarious new life and a rival for the job he had fought to get. Now he saw everything that had happened as inevitable.

'We were meant to find each other, Mich. Why else would we have been thrown together on this job? We fit. Spending the last few weeks with you has been the best time, even though we've both been going through so much. You accepted Ebony, forgave me for being an idiot, and…'

'Broke your nose?' She leaned up on her elbows, dropping a kiss onto the bridge of his still healing nose. 'Where has all this come from? What about the job?'

He dropped a kiss onto her nose, right where she had kissed him. 'The job is beyond our control. Andrew will choose his person, and we will deal with it together. We'll deal with *everything* together.'

* * *

Jacob's body was shielding hers in the dimly lit on-call room. She could feel his heart beating, racing, even as he spoke. Words that she had never expected him to say. Words of feelings and emotion from the man she'd used to mock, the player with pudding.

If Rebecca had been here, they would have had a lot to discuss.

Thinking of her friend for once didn't feel like a stab to the heart, and she found herself feeling glad that he had known her. He got how funny she'd been, how much of a best-friend-shaped hole she had left behind after her death.

She couldn't quite see how it would work—what their life together would look like. But the only thing she knew for sure was that she felt the same, and she wanted to find out the answers to all those questions. With him.

It just seemed too big for the moment.

'Come here,' she said, instead of saying all the things she wanted to say. 'Shut up and kiss me, Jacob.' He tried to speak, but she silenced him with her index finger pushed against his lips. 'Kiss me *now*.'

He reached for her hands and raised both of them above her head on the bedspread. He kissed her then, just once, a small touch of his lips on her forehead, her cheeks, her chin...

'Like this?' he said, pulling down her top a little with his teeth and nibbling along her collarbone. 'Don't you don't want me to ask you how much you want this?'

He mouthed her breast through her clothes and she felt his hot breath blow on her nipple through the material.

'Or this? Don't you don't want me to talk about how this makes me feel?'

He ran a line across the length of her clavicle with his tongue, the two-day stubble on his tired face driving her crazy as he nuzzled against her skin.

'Jacob...' she tried, but he didn't give her a chance to answer.

He claimed her mouth, and all she could do was kiss him back while her head swam. He was all around her: his touch, his scent, the feeling his fingers stirred in her as he slowly pulled off her clothing.

In moments they were naked on top of the covers, their bodies entwined together. She felt as if there was a huge question mark blinking above them, but as he moved inside her the only thing she could think about was saying yes and hang the consequences.

A frantic knocking at the door made them both freeze.

Jacob rolled over to grab the duvet and cover their modesty.

'Who knows you're here?' she whispered to him.

Their lips were almost touching. He'd wrapped himself around her tightly, and she was thrilled by his protective instinct—not that she would let on.

He shook his head. 'I'm not sure. What about you?'

She shrugged. The knock came again.

'Dr Peterson? Dr Peterson?'

It was Francis, a nurse from the ward. He had been looking after Ebony at night.

They both reacted simultaneously.

Michelle grabbed her clothes and ran to the bathroom.

'Ebony. You go. I'll follow.'

As she dressed she heard Jacob answer the door. She couldn't make out the voices, but she knew by instinct that trouble was coming. She shoved her feet into her shoes just as Jacob opened the bathroom door, the duvet only just protecting his modesty.

'Ebony's missing,' he panted. 'She wasn't in the TV room after the movie. She's gone.'

## CHAPTER NINE

MICHELLE WALKED ON to the trauma floor and, sticking two fingers in her mouth, whistled hard. The cacophony of noise from the staff stopped and they all focused on her.

'Listen up! Ebony Peterson is missing. Security have locked down the building and Andrew is going over CCTV footage with the police. Ebony is five years old; she came in with the bus crash. Restrained passenger. Minor injuries. Due to be discharged tomorrow.'

She looked across at Jacob, who was going through the visitors' log with a fine-tooth comb, his phone in his hand. He'd already ruled out Jenny, who was away for the weekend with one of her friends. He had told her she wouldn't have come to take her anyway—she showed little interest in her as it was.

From the look Michelle had seen on Jacob's face when he'd spoken to her on the phone, she thought there wouldn't be any frantic mother-daughter reunion any time soon. She wasn't coming to help.

'Ebony has autism,' she added. 'She isn't good with strangers or unfamiliar surroundings. If you find her, do *not* put hands on. Do not chase her; only take steps to protect where absolutely necessary. You all have Jacob— Dr Peterson's pager. He'll be here in case she returns.'

She checked her watch.

'It's twenty-one seventeen. Ebony was last seen fifteen minutes ago, in the TV room. She wasn't there when staff came to take her back to her bed, and we believe that she's still in the grounds.' She looked at the sea of familiar faces in front of her—people she loved, admired, trusted. 'Ebony is vulnerable, guys. Let's find her—and fast. Move out!'

Jude came over. 'Nice speech, boss. Good to have you here. How can I help?'

Michelle passed her a soft toy—apparently one of Ebony's favourites from home. 'Check the children's ward. She could have gone down there, or if someone has found her they might take her there.'

Jude nodded, glancing back to where Jacob

was sitting on a nurses' station chair with his head in his hands. 'He's in a bad way. You looking after him?'

Something in the tone of her comment made Michelle look at her.

Jude winked. 'It's not the time, but we need to talk, girl. I need details.'

Michelle looked at her open-mouthed. 'How…?'

Jude laughed, just once, before her expression turned back to concerned and professional. 'I've got eyes,' she said. She looked at Jacob, making Michelle turn her head too. 'It can work, Michelle. Don't question it. I'll let you know if I find Ebony.'

Michelle nodded, feeling numb, but Jude was already gone. Her team had scrambled and the place was crawling with medical personnel, all looking for the little girl.

Heading over to Jacob, she pulled up a seat, placing her hand over his. 'We'll find her,' she said, with absolute conviction.

She knew that every single member of staff at St Marshall's would turn over every bedpan and operating room looking for Ebony, and with the hospital on lockdown no one was getting in or out till she was safely back in her father's arms.

'Jacob, did you hear me? We'll find her.'

He didn't say anything, just sat there staring into space. Michelle had never seen him so lost before.

Over his shoulder, she saw Andrew hovering. 'I won't be long. You go and check on the CCTV again—see if you spot anything, okay?'

She beckoned Big Al from Security, who came over to Jacob. She reluctantly let go of his hand and it just fell into his lap. She wanted to throw her arms around him, to kiss his unshed tears away, but it wasn't the time.

'What's wrong?' she said as she reached Andrew. He pulled her to one side.

'We're all locked down, and CCTV doesn't show anyone fitting her description leaving in the last thirty minutes. The police and our security team are going floor to floor. She's here, and we will find her.' Andrew looked over to where Jacob was now pointing to designs of the hospital layout with Big Al and his crew. 'How's he doing?'

Michelle looked at Jacob, so pale, alert but distracted. In another life she might have gone for the jugular right about now. 'He's fine—or as fine as he can be. We have everything in hand. All new traumas have been diverted to other hospitals for now, but discharges are still happening—just taking a bit longer with security at the main doors having to be stepped up.'

Andrew didn't look convinced. He opened and closed his mouth, and she knew he wanted to say something else.

'Andrew, just say it. We don't have time to pussyfoot around.'

'No, you're right.' He gave her one of his trademark thumbs-up, which made him look slightly goofy. 'It's not the time at all. We can speak later. Are you two friends now, or something?'

Michelle couldn't help but think he had more to say, but she had no time to digest it. His 'friends' comment had made her think of something and had given her an idea.

She patted Andrew on the shoulder. 'Something like that, boss…yeah. I gotta go.'

Heading straight over to Jacob, she put her arm on his shoulder, bending close and whispering something in his ear. He looked at her with a spark of hope in his eyes and then the pair of them headed down the corridor, delivering orders to staff on their way.

They were all heading elsewhere, but Michelle hoped with every fibre of her being that her hunch was right. The alternative didn't bear thinking about.

Just past the TV room there was another corridor, sectioned off from patients, which housed the offices, locker rooms and staff rooms for the adjacent departments nearby. Michelle and Jacob headed slowly down this corridor, looking in every room just in case. Nothing.

Soon they reached a locker room, and Michelle paused with her hands on the wooden surface of the door, wanting to give them both a second to catch their breath and offer up a silent prayer. She even spoke to Becks, asking her to give the Big Man Upstairs a nudge in their direction.

Pushing the door open, she held her breath. Jacob pushed past her, shouting his daughter's name, and as Michelle followed him in she hoped to God she hadn't got it wrong.

'Ebony!'

Jacob's joyous voice rang out and he ran to the corner of the room, where Ebony was sitting on a beanbag, her face full of chocolate pudding, a half-eaten pot on her lap.

'Ebony, honey!'

Jacob didn't tell her off, just sat down beside her and pulled her onto his lap. She squirmed a little, freeing her hand enough from her father's embrace to dip her spoon back into the mousse. He checked her over, looking for bruises, injuries, but there was nothing. She was absolutely fine—not a scratch on her.

Michelle felt something on her face, wet and dripping, and when she went to wipe her cheeks she realised she was crying.

'Michelle?'

Jacob was looking at her now, his face full of concern, and Ebony's eyes were tracking her movements as she half ran across the room and threw her arms around them both. Jacob moved till they were all sitting on the oversized beanbag, a huddle of limbs and chocolate pudding.

'You're a good dad, you know?' she said, wiping away her tears of relief. 'I know it must have been hard, but she's adorable. Don't blame yourself for this; you know more than most that things just happen sometimes. She's in good hands with Susan. You were working…saving lives. I'm sure Ebony is proud of her old pops.'

She felt the same sense of pride, looking at him with fresh eyes now that she had all the pieces of the puzzle. She'd been so worried when Ebony had gone missing, and she'd felt something she'd not felt for a while. A rush of protective instinct, a bloom of love.

She cared about Ebony—had got used to seeing the little inquisitive lass around the place. The girl's health and happiness mattered to her, as it obviously did to Jacob. He'd been lost himself, but he'd still found the time to care for her, to be there when she needed him. He and his daughter were partners, in every single sense of the word.

'I get it now,' she said, giving him a look of adoration that made him blush a little.

'Get what?' he asked, dropping kisses on both their heads as though he couldn't quite believe his luck at having the two of them in his arms, safe.

'The pudding. It was all for Ebony, wasn't it? The whole "pudding man" thing?'

Jacob laughed then, and Ebony laughed with him.

Pointing at her dad, she said, as clear as a bell, 'Pudding man Daddy!' She squealed, belly-laughing this time, and touching Michelle's cheek, bringing her in on the joke.

Michelle took her little hand in hers and kissed it. 'Oh, Ebony, that laugh!'

Ebony laughed again, waggling her ears with her hands in response. Jacob followed suit.

And as Michelle grabbed her phone, to call off the alert, they all sat and waggled their ears together, waiting for the others to descend on their little moment. Right now, the three of them were enjoying just being together.

## CHAPTER TEN

WAKING UP ALONE in the on-call room the next morning, Michelle felt she had never slept better. She had fallen asleep feeling content, the demons silent. The elastic band sat on her pile of clothes; her wrists were bare. The sun was low in the sky, peeking through the blinds and warming her skin as the day got started.

She saw from her watch that it was just before morning shift. She had half an hour—and less than two till her meeting with Andrew. For once, though, she found that she didn't want to scramble to her feet and hit the day with a fast pace. Not when the bathroom door had opened and Jacob had come through.

He shuffled into the bed behind her, his body flush against her back. 'What time is it?'

His low, rumbling voice vibrated around her, and he rubbed his stubble on her cheek, making her squirm and feel turned on at the same time.

'Half an hour till hand-over. Ebony okay? You're on all day, aren't you?'

Jacob groaned before answering her question. 'She's fine. The nurses have her—and it looks like Gok Wan came to dress her, judging by the outfit choices and accessories. Why do I do this again?'

He sat up a little as he spoke, his hair in tufts around his head. He looked like a baby monkey, and it made her giggle.

'What?'

He ran a hand through his hair when he caught her looking and she pulled it away, placing it on her breast and moulding his fingers around it. He made a throaty growling sound and squeezed, running his finger over her bare nipple.

'Good morning, Dr Peterson.' She kissed him on the top of his head. He turned his head to claim her mouth, but she blocked him with her finger. 'Morning breath,' she quipped, pretending to cross her eyes.

He raised his brows, wordlessly reaching over to where his lab coat was thrown over the spare bed. Pulling out a pack of mints, he popped one in his mouth, waggling his eyebrows at her suggestively.

'Now, kiss me, woman. That's an order.'

The kisses turned to caresses in record time—even for two world-class trauma medics.

Later, sitting outside Andrew's office, Jacob knew they were both too wound up and worried even to acknowledge anyone who passed them, wishing them good luck. Looking across at Michelle, who looked confident, but was plucking her elastic band like a guitar string, he didn't even want to think about what would happen once the decision was made.

After the last few weeks, it felt so cruel that one little decision could hold so much power over their lives.

Ebony was settled, but fragile still, so much in need of someone to keep the home fires burning safely.

Michelle was in therapy, and it was working, but PTSD was no easy fix. She'd never be the same again. Love was a battlefield, they said, and loving and losing someone right in front of you brought the worst kind of grief. She was a trauma doctor and she'd been right there, and still helpless. Jacob knew from experience that Michelle would never forget that day, and that the memory of it would shape her future career whether she wanted it to or not.

He leaned in to her, whispering into her ear urgently, trying to get his words out before Andrew opened that door. 'You okay? You ready?'

Michelle flicked the band once more and, closing her eyes for a long moment, took a deep breath. 'I hope this works Jacob; it's a risk.'

He smiled at her, hiding his anxiety, showing her he had her back. 'What isn't a risk these days? You took me on, and that's worked out pretty well.'

She rolled her eyes, hiding the elastic band under her sleeve. 'Jury's still out on that one.'

He narrowed his eyes at her. 'You know me, honey. I'm a sure thing when it comes to what I want.'

The door opened. It was show time.

'So...' Andrew started, clearly trying and failing to be a detached professional in this situation.

He looked as if he had been made chief executioner and this was his first day on the job.

If he'd been on a lower floor, he might even have done a bunk out of the office window. Jacob, for one, wouldn't have blamed him. It was a tough time.

'So?' Michelle echoed, leaning forward and picking up one of the iced Danish pastries from a platter on his desk. 'Any coffee?'

Andrew's shoulders dropped a little and he smiled at her. 'It's on the way. I want to talk to you both about the job. I've made a decision.'

Jacob was still standing, leaning against the wall behind her chair. She looked at him. 'Do you want to tell him, or shall I?' she asked.

They were interrupted by Andrew's secretary, bringing in a tray of coffee. They were all left to stare and glare at each other, setting their faces to happy whenever the secretary looked their way.

Jacob felt as if his heart was going to explode out of his chest. Michelle was so damn cool about it, the elastic band hanging loose from her wrist as she ripped into another pastry like a bear with a fresh salmon.

She gave him a look that helped him to find his voice.

*She's in my corner and I'm firmly camped in*

*hers. Stick an I-heart-Michelle flag in me, because I'm home.*

'Andrew, we both want to take the job, so we humbly accept.' He kept his jaw tight, his look professional, steely. 'We do have a few conditions, though.'

'But— But— But…' Andrew started to say. 'You—? Both?'

Jacob could see pound signs and panic flashing up in Andrew's eyes.

'Part-time,' he said, to put him out of his misery. 'I have Ebony, and Michelle is in therapy— as you know.'

He didn't insult Andrew's intelligence; of course he knew the situation. Michelle was far too good a medic to put her patients at risk— intentionally or otherwise.

'We both love this place and we want it to run right. We think if we speak to the investors, show them our plans for the centre, they'll be on board. A once-in-a-lifetime, two-for-one deal.'

The fact that they had acted like a dream duo of medics on that fundraising night had helped them stand out in the crowd, and their investors were all about the 'faces' of the hospital. A short chat with them this morning and now everything was in motion. The investors were interested. They just needed Andrew to sign off.

Even the staff, who had been firmly in two camps—Peterson or Forbes—had come together over the last few days, cemented by Ebony's disappearance and the need to pull together as one.

Andrew, looking once more like a fish out of water, sat back in his swivel chair and poured himself a coffee, slugging it back like a shot.

Michelle winked at Jacob, and he winked right back.

'Go on, then,' Andrew sighed, half laughing, half crying at the thought of the impending paperwork. 'Hit me with it.'

Michelle had poured her own coffee, clearly brought to life with excitement now.

'We want to turn the job into a two-person role,' she said. 'It will mean we can both get the time off that we need and we can run the department better.'

She looked Jacob in the eye, and once more his heart swelled with love.

*This woman, Becks... I can't help but think*

*that you brought us together somehow. So, thank you. This pudding man is ever grateful.*

Clearing his throat, he stood tall and began to speak.

*Here goes. Stay with me, Michelle.*

'We have run our proposal by the investors— a skeleton plan—and not only have they agreed to having us both run the centre, they want to offer us additional funding to run another project.'

Michelle's face dropped, and in a second Jacob knew her shields had gone whizzing back up. He went and stood behind her chair, placing both hands on her shoulders. She reached up and took his hands without thinking.

Andrew's eyes bulged. 'And how did you do *that* in one meeting?'

'A telephone call, actually. Right after the one we made to the Royal.'

Andrew's nostrils flared at Jacob's words. They had always been the rival hospital to St Marshall's, and Andrew's main goal in life was to stay ahead of the opposition.

'The investors didn't realise that both of their potential trauma doctors might be wanting to work elsewhere. They didn't seem keen on us working for the Royal, though, did they, Mich?'

Michelle was enjoying this now—he could tell by her look. It made him stir into life.

*Not now.*

'They weren't exactly doing cartwheels, no,' she replied. 'I think they might just want to keep us here.'

Andrew shook his head slowly, a disbelieving look of realisation spreading across his face. 'Well played. Wish I'd thought of it myself. And the project?' he asked.

Jacob squeezed Michelle's shoulders, once, twice.

*I'm here. No more are you alone.*

'Michelle and I both have overseas trauma experience. We want to help our veterans when they come back home, and since healthcare has suffered so many cuts we plan to run a privately funded post-service clinic for veterans of war. We have half the department heads already clamouring to help, and the nurses are all on board too. We can run it on the site of the old trauma centre, which was earmarked—'

'For storage.' Andrew nodded. 'I get it. Using that space makes sense. But can you do both?

Even with the two of you it will mean long hours, and juggling your personal lives. Can you really work as partners to that extreme?'

Michelle, who had obviously been prepared to fight Andrew on every little point, looked a little blindsided by his easy acceptance. Jacob was ready for it, though, and he recited the words that had been seared on his brain for days.

'Andrew, we *are* partners. In every sense. We can do this—we just need you to give us the chance.'

He half expected Michelle to pull away, to withdraw her hands from his, but she stood up with him.

'He's right, Andrew. I know we didn't get on at first, but things have changed so much.' She looked at her old friend and he smiled at her. 'I've changed. Trauma needs to change too. We're cutting edge here, so why not reach out? Do more? Link our trauma department with helping our armed forces like they help us, going out there every day.' She thought of Kathryn, left without a daughter, herself without a best friend. 'We owe them that, at the very least.'

Andrew leaned forward, resting his elbows on his desk and forming a steeple with his fingers.

*A classic playing for time move*, Jacob thought. *We have him.*

Standing up, Andrew offered his hand to them both. 'Doctors, you have yourself a deal. I'll call the investors now.'

## CHAPTER ELEVEN

'COMING, READY OR NOT!' Jude shouted, sending giggling children scattering in all directions over the grassy sunlit fields around them.

Ebony was one of the loudest, screaming, 'No, Jude, don't find me!' as she grabbed Jacob's hand and took off running.

Jacob was howling with laughter himself, a relaxed figure in jeans and a crisp white shirt.

The opening of the new trauma centre was shaping up to be a day to remember. They had been able to utilise the fields near the hospital grounds, and now a square of beautiful white marquees stood proudly on the green grass that flowed like a carpet beyond them. Music was playing—a local band that Jacob had organised—family-friendly hits that everyone, young and old could enjoy together, and the children were busy playing hide and seek with Jude, but there were other activities dotted around too—

most of them down to the genius of Ebony and her dear old dad.

When she was settled and happy Ebony uncurled, going from being a nervous little scrap of a girl to a very clever, happy little brainbox. Michelle was surprised by her every time she saw her, and seeing Jacob with her was showing her a whole other side to her former rival.

'Everything running smoothly, I assume?' Andrew came to her side as she watched the children, passing her a glass of Bucks Fizz. 'The investors are loving this fun day for the opening. How did you know they all had kids?'

She nodded towards Jacob with a smile. He was lying on the grass, getting tickled by half a dozen very excited kids. 'Jacob did some research. Worked out well, didn't it?'

Looking around at the milling crowd, all enjoying being together, she knew Andrew had to agree. All the patients who were well enough to leave the wards were sitting in the sun, spending time with their loved ones, and people had come from far and wide to mark this special occasion.

Michelle spotted someone she recognised in the crowd. Excusing herself from Andrew, she headed over, self-consciously smoothing down the maxi-dress and jewelled sandals Jacob had helped her pick out for the day. She didn't feel quite herself, dressed like this, but she wanted to look nice and make an effort for the special day.

A woman on her own had come from the hospital and was walking towards the refreshment tent, her head turning this way and that. She was looking for *her*.

Michelle took a deep breath, using the clasped hands and deep breathing exercises her therapist had been teaching her. She had a few elastic bands in her bag—just in case. Plus, she had a hot surgeon boyfriend who had a pile of them in his pocket at all times. She loved him for that, even though she pretended not to notice. Jacob had surprised her in so many ways...

'Hello,' she said, stopping a short distance away from the woman. 'Thank you for coming.'

Kathryn Hughes looked like a carbon copy of her daughter—right down to the eyes and the easy smile. It was a shock to Michelle's system, but she recovered well.

'Thank you for inviting me,' Kathryn said in

her usual warm way. 'How are you? You look well.'

Michelle had a million replies in her head.

*Thanks, so do you. I picked my outfit especially to meet you. I miss your daughter. Thanks for bringing such an amazing person into the world.*

Nothing seemed right—or enough. So Michelle drew her into a tight hug instead, and the two of them clung to each other, lost in their own world together.

'I'm sorry I wasn't there after the funeral,' Michelle whispered to her. 'I wanted to be—I really did.'

Kathryn squeezed her tighter, stroking her long flowing hair with her hand. A mother for ever, but now her arms were empty.

'You did what you could, my darling I know it's been hard for you too.' She pulled away a little, smoothing the wavy auburn hair away from Michelle's face and taking her in. 'Are you getting help?'

'Straight to the point, as always,' Michelle replied. 'I am getting help—I promise.'

Kathryn's face relaxed a little, her smile a bit brighter.

'Don't worry about me, Kathryn. I'm good. And I have someone for you to meet.'

Jacob, whom she knew had been watching the whole exchange, came walking over with Ebony holding his hand. Ebony was wearing a cream tulle dress, now streaked with grass stains, and Jacob had bright green patches on his jeans from diving onto the grass.

'Look at you two!' Michelle said, laughing. 'I don't envy your dry cleaner.'

Jacob grinned, flashing her one of his sexy looks. 'It's totally worth it. Right, Ebs?'

Ebony giggled. 'Totally! Who's this lady?'

Michelle had been working out how to introduce the pair, but Kathryn was already kneeling.

'My name is Kathryn. I'm a friend of Michelle's.' She held out her hand, and Ebony high-fived her.

Kathryn laughed—a carefree, happy laugh that startled Michelle. She hadn't heard it in so long.

'Sorry,' Jacob said, taking Kathryn's hand and shaking it himself. 'We're working on greeting people. I'm Jacob, one of the doctors here, and this is Ebony, my daughter.'

'I love a good high-five,' Kathryn said to Ebony kindly. 'Makes saying hello fun. Do you like the new hospital?' she asked.

Ebony nodded, looking around her, already distracted by the stalls.

Jacob pulled a coin out of his pocket, giving it to her. 'See Jude over there?' he asked.

Jude was standing with a group of children near the ice-cream van they had hired, and she spotted them, waving at Ebony.

'You go get an ice cream. I'll come in a minute.'

Ebony seized the coin and took off, her cream dress billowing behind her like a cape as she ran to the others.

'She's beautiful,' Kathryn said as the three of them watched the little girl leave.

'Oh, she's a handful, believe me,' said Jacob.

She had her moments, Michelle thought. But she had recovered from the accident. Riding in the car had become a bit of an experience, but with headphones and the latest Disney soundtrack they'd managed to get her mobile again.

'So, Jacob, I hear you knew my daughter?' Kathryn said.

As Jacob looked in panic at a very amused Michelle, Andrew's voice rang out over the lawn.

'It's time,' Michelle said, and gathering her whole crew together, Kathryn at her side, she walked across the grass to the main marquee, which was positioned right near the entrance to the new trauma centre, and the building that housed the secret project they planned to break ground on in a few short weeks' time.

Just as they were entering the tent Michelle felt a little hand brush against her fingers, gripping them tightly. Little Ebony looked up at her before returning to her ice cream, and Michelle winked. Ebony did it back, with both eyes, making her laugh.

The guests were all taking their seats in the white wooden chairs that had been put into rows, facing a stage with a podium, which Andrew was now standing at. He was dressed in a lightweight linen suit, and the trustees of the hospital were sitting behind him, chatting amongst themselves.

Michelle and her party sat in the reserved back row. Everything had been planned to the last detail, and they had put so much work into today. Now it was here, Michelle couldn't help but worry about it not going well.

'Hey,' Jacob said, looking at Ebony, who was talking to Jude and Kathryn as they waited. His dark hair looked so deep and rich against the white backdrop of the marquee. 'Stop worrying. We've covered everything. We've rocked it, and today's going to be amazing.'

Michelle's heart fluttered at his words, but she didn't tell him that. Not this time. She had to have *some* mystique left—despite the fact that since Ebony had arrived at the hospital they had barely spent a moment apart.

'I know, but—'

'But nothing. Just enjoy it.' He patted his pocket. 'You need a band?'

She shook her head. 'No, I'll be fine.'

Everyone was assembled, and the crowd fell silent as Andrew started speaking.

'I am very happy to see so many people here at St. Marshall's today, to celebrate the opening of our new trauma centre. Surrey, as you know, has a fantastic community spirit, and seeing you all here today, getting involved, has been amazing. We are now officially a top trauma centre—and, thanks to the generosity of our trustees and investors, we are delighted to announce that on the site of the old trauma ward we will be developing a veterans' treatment centre, specialising in trauma aftercare, orthopaedics and prosthetics, as well as bespoke mental health services to help with the after-effects of close combat and PTSD.'

His eyes locked with Michelle's and she nodded, spurring him on. The flashes of cameras all around him told her that the press were lapping it up. All good publicity—which meant more awareness, more people they could help. She looked across at Kathryn nervously, but she was paying attention to Andrew, unaware of Michelle's panic.

'And it is down to two doctors—two magnificent former frontline medics—that this centre is going to happen. So huge thanks to Dr Michelle Forbes and Dr Jacob Peterson, who will be around today to answer any questions you might have. They know their stuff, so do say hello, look around our new trauma centre, see the plans for the old site. Have fun with your families today, here at St Marshall's. And Mayor Atkinson will now open the centre.'

The Mayor of the county stepped forward. 'Thank you, Dr Chambers, and thank you, everyone, for coming out to support our hospital today. Without further ado, I officially declare the Rebecca Hughes Trauma Centre…' He reached for the rope which had been set up to pull a tarp from the side of the building. It fell away, revealing Rebecca's name up there on the wall. *'Open!'*

The crowd all gasped and cheered, clapping and standing up as they saw the building unveiled for the first time.

Michelle closed her eyes. *Goodbye, my dearest friend. I love you and I will never forget you.* When she opened her eyes Kathryn was standing there, tears in her eyes.

'Kathryn, I—'

Michelle's words were crushed in Kathryn's embrace as the woman threw her arms around Michelle, holding her tight.

'I can't believe you did this—not only getting in touch, but—' Kathryn's voice broke as she looked at her daughter's name, standing out clear and proud for all to see.

'I loved her too,' Michelle said, trying not to

break down herself. 'I feel like she's always with me, and now everyone will know her name.'

Kathryn nodded, too choked up from crying to speak. She mouthed *Thank you*, and Michelle kissed her cheek as she took out a tissue and wiped at her eyes.

'It was down to Jacob,' Michelle admitted, when they had both managed to stop crying enough to speak properly. 'It was his idea— the centre name, I mean.'

Both women looked across the lawn to where Jacob was now playing aeroplanes with some of the children. Ebony was on his back, like a baby monkey, his arms were outstretched, and he was twisting and turning his body around, chasing the kids and making them all laugh.

Ebony laughed the loudest, and she looked so happy, her little face quite recovered from the cuts from the crash.

Kathryn smiled wistfully as she watched them, and Michelle saw her emotions change as she observed.

'He's a good man,' Kathryn said after a time. 'He's a good influence on you too.'

Michelle blushed.

'Oh, I see you. missy. Don't be shy. You never looked like this around Scott. He was nice, and everything, but I have a feeling you've met your match here. Life's too short not to grab a bit of happiness now and again. God knows, I wish I'd grabbed a little more.'

Michelle was about to ask what she was talking about when Andrew headed over.

'Michelle, I'm sorry but we have incoming trauma.' He smiled politely at Kathryn and she waved Michelle away.

'You go, pet. I'm fine here. Andrew, do you fancy getting a drink with me?'

Andrew, ever the host, bowed theatrically, holding out his arm for his new companion. 'I would be delighted, Kathryn. Let's go.'

Andrew nodded to Michelle and the pair headed slowly over to the refreshment tent.

Michelle looked for Jacob, but he and the children had gone.

Heading into the trauma centre, she looked above her head at the new sign and marvelled at how at home Rebecca's name looked up there. She would come through these doors every day now, and she couldn't think of a better way to remember her beautiful friend.

'Hey, no slacking now you're a part-timer.' Jacob came up beside her, discarding his tie on the nearest planter as they walked through the main doors of their new domain. 'Where's the fire?'

'Incoming. You get a page?'

He shook his head. 'Nope. Andrew mentioned it and I just came to help. He's with Ebony and Kathryn—she's taken a real shine to our girl.'

*Our girl.*

Michelle didn't react, but her heart felt as though it was lit up like a glow-worm in her chest.

They both went in and Wendy and Imogen, the two trauma nurses on duty that day, galvanised themselves as soon as they set eyes on the doctors, heading straight for them and giving them the lowdown on the casualties.

'Okay,' Jacob said, after hearing about the injuries of the five patients who were en route. 'Cross-check bloods, set up crash carts in Beds Two and Three, get Ortho and Paediatrics down here, and we'll go and change.'

'What about the party?' Wendy asked.

'The party's here!' Michelle said, slipping

off her sandals as she walked. 'We'll let them get on with that while we show them why this trauma centre is worth all that cash!'

# CHAPTER TWELVE

*Two years later...*

MICHELLE WALKED INTO the hospital chapel, her dress swishing as she stepped up to the altar slowly. Her legs felt shaky, unsure. *Damn heels.* She never did quite feel herself in them, but needs must…

Heading to the candles, she lit one and looked up to the ceiling. 'Well?' she said, laughing even as she wiped a tear away from her face with a gloved hand. 'Here we are. What do you think?'

She walked in a slow circle, showing off her outfit.

'Not bad for a former desert-dweller, eh?' She sat down carefully on the front pew, watching the candlelight flicker in the room. 'I know you think I need a minute, but I don't. I'm absolutely fine. Honestly.'

The room stayed silent, and Michelle rolled her eyes.

'Okay, so maybe just a minute. It's a lot, you know?' She cocked her head to one side, as though she was listening. 'Yeah, yeah, I'm going.'

'You about done?' a voice said from behind her.

Turning, she saw Jude and Andrew standing there, arm in arm. Jude did not look happy.

'You've ruined my make-up job!'

She came running at her, grabbing cosmetics from her tiny purse and getting to work on her face as Andrew looked on.

'Talking to Becks?' he said softly, nodding his head towards the candles.

'I gave her your love,' Michelle replied, squeezing his arm. 'How is he?' she asked nervously.

Andrew, ever the diplomat, shrugged easily. 'He's fine. Everything's good.'

Jude turned to glare at him. 'Andrew, don't lie to the girl.' She turned and gave Michelle a conspiratorial look. 'He's vomited twice—once in the nurses' station bin. It ain't pretty. We'd better not keep him waiting.'

Michelle nodded. 'Lead the way.'

Heading out of the hospital, arm in arm with her friends, colleagues who had borne witness to her past, her present and her future, she was grateful. Grateful that they'd stuck by her, been stubborn enough to hang on in there with her, even when she had tried to drive them away.

Heading to The Pub on the Corner, on Andrew's arm, she took a deep breath and started to walk inside. The pub had been transformed, with white organza and satin draped over the walls, the chair-backs trimmed with gold ribbon, the tables all moved to form a makeshift aisle.

Michelle didn't see the congregation there—she only saw him. Dressed in a grey suit, his collar constricted by a blue cravat. She locked eyes with him and floated the rest of the way.

Ebony was standing off to one side, and she stopped in front of her. 'Here you go, darling,' she said, passing over her tied bouquet of calla lilies.

'You look beautiful, Mummy.' Ebony beamed.

Her dress was a smaller version of Michelle's, her sparkling green eyes a present from the man she was about to marry—her daddy.

Michelle pulled her close and Ebony flinched. 'Your make-up!' she whispered. She cupped a hand around her mouth and whispered in her new mother's ear. 'Auntie Jude says she'll paint you like Bobo the clown if you mess it up again.'

Michelle made a little *'whoops'* noise, and the pair of them laughed.

'Love you,' Michelle said to Ebony, the daughter she had taken on as her own, whom she loved to the ends of the earth.

Her real mother had stepped aside long ago, giving them her blessing, and Michelle couldn't help but think that she *was* her mother now. The one who would be there, no matter what. Even a top-class surgeon knew that it wasn't all about blood. Ebony had people who put her first, people who cared. That bonded them as parents. Their love for Ebony and their care for her needs and wants.

'Love you too,' Ebony whispered back, dropping a little kiss on Michelle's nose before heading back to stand with Jude.

She walked over to Jacob, Andrew dropping a kiss on her cheek before going to sit with Wendy and the others.

Jacob looked across at her, as the pair of them stood toe to toe once more.

'You look utterly beautiful,' he said, a hint of wonder in his voice. 'I love you so much.'

She beamed at him, feeling the sting of tears in her eyes but not caring who saw them this time. She was happy—truly happy for the first time in such a long time.

She saw Kathryn, sitting with the rest of their friends and giving her a watery smile before dabbing at her eyes. The friends comforted her, making her laugh. Friends who were all family now. Ride or die.

Looking out across the little pub, she saw the board. Lucas smiled out from the wall of faces, right next to a new addition or two. The faces of some of the veterans who had come to their centre for help and found new purpose in their lives, children they had saved, families they had helped repair, one kind word and dedicated treatment plan at a time.

In the centre of the board another picture was pinned up. A photo from last month—one that they had hoped for but hadn't expected. The picture had been taken at home—Jacob's home. *Their* home now. They were sitting on the sofa.

She remembered Ebony calling Jacob to sit down and open his present.

'A frame! Wow, cool!' he'd exclaimed, opening the box face down in his excitement, spurred on by Ebony's loud and excited cries.

'Open it, Daddy, open it quick! I can't wait any more!'

Ebony had squashed into Michelle's side on the couch and they had both sat and watched his face as he'd turned the frame over. It was then that they'd taken the photo.

It showed his surprised expression as he held the frame up, saw the monochrome sonogram picture filling the glass. Ebony's fists were in the air, her face scrunched up in happiness, and Michelle was gazing at her growing family with a serene expression. Her favourite photo and it was here. Here to witness the final piece of the puzzle.

'Where did you go?' Jacob leaned in as the registrar started speaking, his brows knitted in concern. 'You okay?'

He put his hand on her stomach instinctively, and she covered it with her own.

'I'm fine. Happy. I love you.'

He squeezed her fingers between his. 'Kinda

glad to hear that—not going to lie. I even threw up earlier.'

The registrar was looking at them a little quizzically now, but they smiled at him, and Jacob lowered his voice when he started to speak again.

'I have to warn you, though. I have a hot date later.'

He looked at her with his emerald eyes, and she had to concentrate for a second to stop her legs from buckling beneath her.

'That's fine,' she said nonchalantly. 'I have a hot doctor waiting for me in the on-call room anyway.'

His eyes flashed with challenge and her heart and her libido soared. Even here, preparing to commit to each other for life, they were still *them*. Messy. Hot-headed. Unconventional. Perfectly imperfect and blissfully happy.

'You won't get far in that dress, I can tell you,' he growled.

The registrar rolled his eyes, not missing a syllable.

'Anything can happen in Trauma—you know the risks.'

She did, she thought. She knew the risks—and the lows.

Looking at her husband-to-be, the father of her unborn child and of her daughter who looked just like him, she smiled.

'Bring it on, player,' she said, wrinkling her nose at him.

The nod to his old life held no barb for them now. It was a love token, an acknowledgement of their shared past, their entwined future.

'Woman,' he said, ignoring the registrar's pleading eyes. 'Bring. It. On.'

\* \* \* \* \*

# LET'S TALK

## Romance

For exclusive extracts, competitions and special offers, find us online:

**f** facebook.com/millsandboon

**⊙** @millsandboonuk

**🐦** @millsandboon

Or get in touch on 0844 844 1351*

For all the latest titles coming soon, visit millsandboon.co.uk/nextmonth

*Calls cost 7p per minute plus your phone company's price per minute access charge